Back by Popular Demand

A collector's edition of favorite titles from
one of th—
authors—
back thes—
them a—

COLLECTOR'S EDITION

A GENTLE AWAKENING
RING IN A TEACUP
OFF WITH THE OLD LOVE
THE MOON FOR LAVINIA
PINEAPPLE GIRL
BRITANNIA ALL AT SEA
CAROLINE'S WATERLOO
HEAVEN AROUND THE CORNER
THE LITTLE DRAGON
THE SILVER THAW
ALL ELSE CONFUSION
NEVER SAY GOODBYE
THE PROMISE OF HAPPINESS
A GIRL TO LOVE
A DREAM CAME TRUE
NEVER TOO LATE

HARLEQUIN®

Betty Neels spent her childhood and youth in Devonshire before training as a nurse and midwife. She was an army nursing sister during the war, married a Dutchman and subsequently lived in Holland for fourteen years. She now lives with her husband in Dorset, and has a daughter and grandson. Her hobbies are reading, animals, old buildings and, of course, writing. Betty started to write on retirement from nursing, incited by a lady in a library bemoaning the lack of romantic novels.

Mrs. Neels is always delighted to receive fan letters, but would truly appreciate it if they could be directed to Harlequin Mills & Boon Ltd., 18-24 Paradise Road, Richmond, Surrey, TW9 1SR, England.

Books by Betty Neels

HARLEQUIN ROMANCE
3355—DEAREST LOVE
3363—A SECRET INFATUATION
3371—WEDDING BELLS FOR BEATRICE
3389—A CHRISTMAS WISH
3400—WAITING FOR DEBORAH
3415—THE BACHELOR'S WEDDING
3435—DEAREST MARY JANE
3454—FATE TAKES A HAND
3467—THE RIGHT KIND OF GIRL
3483—THE MISTLETOE KISS
3492—MARRYING MARY
3512—A KISS FOR JULIE
3527—THE VICAR'S DAUGHTER
3537—ONLY BY CHANCE

BETTY NEELS

BRITANNIA ALL AT SEA

COLLECTOR'S EDITION

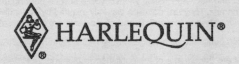

HARLEQUIN®

TORONTO • NEW YORK • LONDON
AMSTERDAM • PARIS • SYDNEY • HAMBURG
STOCKHOLM • ATHENS • TOKYO • MILAN • MADRID
PRAGUE • WARSAW • BUDAPEST • AUCKLAND

ISBN 0-373-63106-5

BRITANNIA ALL AT SEA

First North American Publication 1999.

Printed in U.S.A.

CHAPTER ONE

THE SLUICE ROOM at the end of Men's Surgical at St Jude's Hospital was deplorably out of date; built in Victorian times, it was always damp and chilly, its white-tiled walls and heavy earthenware sinks doing nothing to alleviate its dismal appearance. The plumbing was complicated and noisy and the bedpan washer made a peculiar clanging noise, but because some time in the distant future the hospital was to be re-sited and become a modern showpiece with every conceivable mod con the architect and Hospital Committee could think of, the antediluvian conditions which at present existed were overlooked—not by the nursing staff, of course, who had to cope with them and voiced their complaints, singly and in groups, round the clock. And a lot of good it did them, for no one listened.

But the occupants of the sluice room weren't aware of its shortcomings; the younger, smaller girl was crying her eyes out by the sink and her companion, a tall, splendidly built girl, was deep in thought, her large brown eyes gazing unseeingly at the conglomeration of pipes on the wall before her.

She waited patiently until the crying had eased a little before speaking.

'Don't cry any more, Dora...' She had a soft, unhurried voice. 'I'll see Sister the moment the round's over—I'll not have you take the blame for something Delia has done—and knows she's done, too. I know you don't like telling on anyone and if Sister hadn't been in such a fuss about the round, she might have listened. Of course, it would happen on this very morning just when everything had to be just so for this wretched professor, but you're not in the least to blame, so dry your eyes, go down the back stairs and have your coffee and tidy up that face. I'll think of something to tell Sister if she wants to know where you are. She won't though, not while Mr Hyde and this tiresome old gent are here.'

She leaned across and switched off the bedpan washer so that there was more or less silence save for the gurgling of the pipes. But not quite silence; a faint noise behind her caused her to turn her head and look behind her. There was someone standing in the doorway, watching her, a very large man with grizzled hair and pale blue eyes, his undoubtedly handsome features marred by a look of annoyance.

'Lost?' she asked him kindly. 'Everyone makes the mistake of coming up these stairs, but I'm afraid you're out of luck; you won't be able to go into the ward until the round's over and that will be at least an hour. Look, Nurse is going down to her coffee— if you go with her, she'll show you the front stairs. There's a waiting room on the landing—I'll let you know the minute they've gone. Have you come to see someone special?'

He regarded her frowningly. 'Yes. Er—Staff Nurse, I presume?'

'That's right. Sister will know about you, I expect. Now if you run along...'

Perhaps it wasn't the best way of putting it, she thought; one didn't tell giants of six feet something and broad with it to run along, but he had no need to look so unsmiling, she had done the best she could to help him. She nodded to the little nurse, who gave a final sniff and managed a very small smile. 'There's a good girl,' said her champion, and put a hand to her cap to make sure that it sat straight on her crown of dark hair as she made for the door. The man didn't move, so she was forced to stop.

'What is your name?' he asked.

'My name?' She was vaguely surprised at the question, but if telling him was going to make him go the quicker, then she might as well do so.

'Smith—Britannia Smith.' She smiled fleetingly and he stood aside. 'Goodbye. Nurse Watts, make sure that this gentleman gets the right stairs, won't you?'

She watched him shrug his shoulders and follow the little nurse down the stairs before she went back into the ward.

It was as old-fashioned as the sluice, with a row of beds on either side and because it was take-in week, three beds down the middle as well. Britannia sped up its length to where Sister Mack, the Surgical Registrar, the surgical houseman, a worried bunch of medical students attached to Mr Hyde's firm, the lady Social Worker, and the senior physiotherapist had grouped themselves, awaiting the great man. The group dissolved and then reformed with Mr Hyde as its hub as she reached them, in time to hear his measured tones voice the opinion that Professor Luitingh van Thien should be joining them at any moment. 'I take it that everything is in readiness, Sister?' he asked, with no idea of it being otherwise.

Sister Mack shot a lightning glance at Britannia, who shook her head. She had been on a swift foray to see if anything could be done to recover at least some of the specimens and while doing so had discovered poor Dora. Sister Mack looked thunderous, but as Britannia saw that look several times a day, she could ignore it and turned her intention instead to the third-year nurse, Delia Marsh, standing there like an innocent angel, she thought indignantly, letting a timid creature like Dora take the blame. She gave the girl a cool thoughtful look and was glad to

see that she had her worried; her pretty mouth
curved just a little downwards in sympathy for Dora
and then rounded itself into a surprised O, while
consternation and horror showed plain on her lovely
face.

The group had increased by one; the man who
had been in the sluice—standing behind everyone
else, just inside the ward doors, surveying her down
his arrogant nose with the hint of a sardonic smile.
Sister Mack looked round then, and if Britannia
hadn't been so taken up with her own feelings, she
might have been amused at that lady's reaction, for
her somewhat hatchet features broke into the ingra-
tiating smile which Sister Mack reserved for those
of importance, and there was no getting away from
the fact that the man looked important, although not
consciously so, Britannia had to concede him that.
The party re-grouped itself once more, this time
with Mr Hyde and his companion wandering off in
the direction of the first bed with Sister Mack hard
on their heels. Britannia gave a soundless chuckle
at the imperious wave she gave to the rest of them
to keep at a respectable distance. After all, they
rarely saw anyone quite as exquisite on the ward,
and Sister Mack considered that she should have the
lion's share of him. And that suited Britannia; with
any luck she would be able to avoid having to speak
to either Mr Hyde or the visitor; she was merely

there as Sister's right hand, to pass forms, offer notes and whisper in Sister's ear any titbit of information she might have overlooked.

She wished she wasn't such a tall girl, for she stood out in the group, and she sighed with relief when the Registrar, edging his way along to join his chief by the bedside, paused beside her. 'And what hit you?' he wanted to know. 'Our professor looks the type to turn any girl's head and here's our gorgeous Britannia all goggle-eyed at the sight of him—anyone would think he had a squint and big ears!'

Britannia spoke earnestly in a thread of a whisper. 'Fred, he was in the sluice just now—he'd come up the staircase and I sent him all the way back and told him to come up the front stairs and wait until the round was over...'

Fred gave a snort of laughter which he turned into a fit of coughing as the two consultants turned round with an impatient: 'Come along, Fred—' from Mr Hyde. The visiting professor said nothing, only raked Britannia with a leisurely look from half-closed eyes. She wondered uneasily if he had heard what she had said and then, obedient to an urgent signal from Sister Mack, slipped behind her and bent her head to receive whatever it was her superior wished to say. 'Nurse Watts—where is she, Staff Nurse? I have not yet told Mr Hyde about the specimens.' She shuddered strongly. 'When I do so, I wish Nurse to be here so that she may admit her carelessness.'

Britannia bit back all the things she would have liked to have said; Sister Mack had been nursing for a good many years now, but apparently she still hadn't learnt that junior nurses could be admonished for their errors in the privacy of Sister's office, but in public they were to be protected, covered up for, backed up...

'I sent her for coffee,' she said with calm.

'You what...? Staff Nurse Smith, sometimes you take too much upon yourself! Why?'

'She didn't do it.'

Sister Mack went a pale puce. 'Of course she did it—anyway, she didn't say a word when I accused her.'

'That's why, Sister—she was too frightened to.'

Sister Mack eyed Britannia with dislike. 'We will discuss this later.' Her expression changed to one of smiling efficiency as she became aware that the two consultants had finished their low-voiced conversation and were looking at them both.

The patient in the first bed was a double inguinal hernia and nicely on the mend—a few minutes' chat sufficed to allay his dark suspicions that Mr Hyde had removed most of his insides without telling him, and they moved to the second bed; a young man

who had been in a motor crash and had ruptured his
liver; Mr Hyde had removed most of the offending
organ, since it was no longer of any use, and his
patient was making a slow recovery—too slow, explained Mr Hyde to his colleague. The two of them
muttered and mumbled together and finally Mr Hyde
enquired: 'The specimen from this lad, Sister? Both
I and Professor Luitingh van Thien wish to examine
it—the blood-clotting time is of great importance...'
He meandered on for a few moments while Sister
Mack's complexion took a turn for the worse and
Britannia prayed that Dora wouldn't come tearing
back too soon. The nasty silence was broken by the
visiting professor. A nice voice, Britannia considered, even though it had a pronounced drawl: 'I understand that the specimens are not available.'

She shot him a look of dislike; if he was going
to sneak on poor Dora in front of everyone, she for
her part would never forgive him—an absurd re-
solve; consultant surgeons were unlikely to be af-
fected by the feelings of a mere staff nurse. But he
wasn't going to sneak. Sister Mack, interrupting him
willy-nilly, declared furiously: 'The nurse responsible isn't here; my staff nurse has seen fit to send her
to coffee...'

His cold eyes held Britannia's warm brown ones
for a moment and then settled on a point a little
above Sister Mack's shoulder. 'I have it on good

authority that Nurse Watts wasn't responsible for the error,' he pointed out in a silky voice. 'I suggest that the matter be looked into and dealt with after the round.' He turned to Mr Hyde. 'I'm sure you will forgive me for saying this, but I happen to have been personally involved...'

Mr Hyde, not very quick to catch on, observed gamely: 'Oh, certainly, my dear chap. We can make do with the notes.' His eyes suddenly lighted on Britannia. 'You know who did it?' he asked. And when she said 'Yes, sir,' he went on, 'And of course, you don't intend to tell me.'

She smiled at him. 'That's right, sir.'

He nodded. 'I like loyalty. I daresay you can get fresh specimens, Sister?'

Sister Mack, quite subdued, muttered something or other and Britannia took the opportunity of putting the next case papers into her hands. The quicker the round got back into its old routine, the better. She looked up and found the professor's eye on her once more and this time, because she was so relieved that he had held his tongue, and at the same time stood up for little Dora, she essayed a smile. His eyes became, if anything, even colder, his fine mouth remained in an unrelenting straight line; he didn't like her. She removed her own smile rapidly and frowned instead.

The next patient, fortunately, was an irascible old

gentleman who had a great deal to say for himself, and as the professor's face was a new one and he looked important, he was able to air his opinion of hospitals, doctors, the nursing staff and the Health Service in general, at some length. Mr Hyde, who had heard it all before, listened with veiled impatience and said 'Yes, yes,' at intervals, not wishing to offend the old man who had, after all, been something important in the War Office in his heyday, but the professor heard him out with great courtesy, even giving the right answers and making suitable comments from time to time so that when at last the diatribe came to an end, the speaker added a corollary to the effect that the professor was a man of sense and might do worse than join the hospital staff. Whereupon Mr Hyde pointed out that his colleague was only paying them a brief visit on his way to Edinburgh and had work enough in his own country. 'A distinguished member of our profession,' he added generously.

'A foreigner,' remarked his patient with a touch of asperity, and then added kindly: 'But his English is excellent.'

The professor thanked him gravely, expressed the wish that he would soon be on his feet again, and with Mr Hyde beside him, wandered on to the next bed. The round was uneventful for the next half a dozen beds; it was when they reached the young man in the corner bed as they started on the second side that interest quickened. He was a very ill young man, admitted only a few days previously, and it became apparent that this was the patient in whom the professor was interested—indeed, intended to operate upon that very afternoon. 'Hydatid cysts,' explained Mr Hyde to his audience, 'diagnosed by means of Casoni's intradermal test—the local and general reaction are very marked.' He signed to Britannia to turn back the bed-clothes and began to examine the patient while he murmured learnedly about rupture, peritonitis and severe anaphylaxis. The professor agreed, nodding his handsome head and adding a few telling words of his own, then said at length: 'We are unable to establish eosinophilia, but the X-rays confirm the cysts, I take it?'

Britannia, on the alert, produced the films with all the aplomb of a first-class conjuror getting a rabbit from a hat and obligingly held them up for viewing while the surgeons, this time with the registrar in attendance, peered and commented. 'Yes, well,' observed the professor at length, 'should you feel that I could help in any way...'

Mr Hyde took him up smartly: 'This afternoon?' He turned to include Sister Mack. 'Could that be arranged, Sister? Shall we say half past two in main theatre? He will go to ICU from theatre and I shall want a responsible nurse to look after him here.' His eye lighted upon Britannia. 'Staff Nurse Smith, perhaps.'

Which would mean that Britannia would have to forgo her evening off duty and, worse, Sister Mack would have to stay on and do her Staff Nurse's work. 'Certainly, sir,' said Britannia, not looking at her superior. She had been going out with Doctor Ross, the Medical Registrar, and now she would have to explain. David was impatient of interference with his wishes; he had booked two seats for the latest musical and the forgoing of a pleasant evening was going to put him out—perhaps a good thing, she decided; he had become a little possessive just lately...

The round rambled on, with frequent pauses while Mr Hyde and his companion murmured, occasionally drawing Sister Mack into their discussion and asking Fred for his opinion, invariably pausing too to say a few appropriate words to the occupants of the beds. At the last bed, Britannia nodded to the ward orderly, peering at them through the glass window of the door; it would never do for the coffee tray in Sister's office not to be there and ready. Not everyone had coffee, of course, only Sister Mack and the consultants and Fred; no one else was considered eligible. Britannia, used to Sister Mack's little ways, despatched the houseman and the students to the kitchen for refreshment and retired to the linen cupboard where Bridget, the ward maid, would have put a tray for her. But before she went she beckoned Delia Marsh to her.

'Before you go to coffee,' she said without heat, 'you will find Dora and apologise, and when you have had your coffee you will report to Sister and tell her that the error was yours, not hers. And I advise you not to do anything like that again. You're in your third year and you should know better.' She nodded dismissal. 'Dora will be back from her coffee, tidying beds.'

The linen cupboard was cosily warm and the frosted glass of its narrow window shut out the grey November morning. Britannia made herself comfortable on a laundry basket and poured her coffee. Bridget was one of the many people in the hospital who liked her; the coffee was hot and milky and two biscuits had been sneaked out of Sister's tin. Britannia munched and swallowed and thought in a vague way about Professor Luitingh van Thien; an ill-tempered man, and arrogant, she considered, then looked up in astonishment as he opened the door and walked in. And over and above that, she discovered with an almighty shock, the man she wished to marry; she had been in and out of love quite a few times, as any healthy-minded girl of twenty-four or so would, but never had she felt like this. Nevertheless, all she said in a mild voice was: 'You should have knocked, Professor.'

The cold eyes studied hers. 'Why?'

She said with some asperity: 'Manners.'

His thick dark brows rose, and then: 'But I have none,' and he went on deliberately, 'I am getting on for forty, unmarried, rich and something of a hermit; I need please no one.'

'How very sad,' observed Britannia with sincerity. 'Did you want something?'

The lids drooped over his eyes. 'Yes. I also wish to ask you a question. Why Britannia?'

She took a sip of her cooling coffee and stared at him over the mug's rim. 'My parents decided that with a name like Smith they should—should compensate me.'

He broke into such a roar of laughter that she exclaimed: 'Oh, hush, do—if Sister hears you she'll be in to see...'

His brows rose again. 'Chance acquaintances over a cup of coffee?'

'Put like that it sounds very respectable, but it wouldn't do, you know. Visiting professors and staff nurses don't meet in linen cupboards.'

'You flatter yourself, Miss Smith. I cannot recall inviting you to meet me.'

She took another sip of coffee. 'Very prickly,' she observed, 'but I quite see why. There's no need for you to stay,' she added kindly, 'I've answered your question.' He looked so surprised that she went on: 'I'm sure that no one speaks to you like that, but it won't harm you, you know.'

He smiled, and she wasn't sure if she liked the smile. 'I stand corrected, don't I?' He put a large square hand on the door. 'And talking of manners, you didn't offer me coffee, Miss Smith.'

'You've just had it,' she pointed out, and added: 'sir.'

'Yes. A cup of vilely brewed liquid, curdled by Sister Mack's conversation. What an unkind woman!' He eyed the almost empty coffee pot as he spoke and Britannia said with real sympathy:

'The kitchen maid makes super coffee—I always have it alone on round days. I enjoyed mine.'

He opened the door. 'Heartless girl,' he remarked coldly, and went out.

Britannia poured herself the last of the coffee. She had forgotten to apologise for sending him out of the sluice, but her whole mind had been absorbed by her sudden uprush of feeling when he had come in so unexpectedly. She frowned, worrying that she would never have the chance to do so now—she wasn't likely to see him again, at least not to speak to. 'And that's negative thinking, my girl,' she admonished herself out loud. 'If you want to see him again, you must work at it.'

A heartening piece of advice, which she knew quite well was quite hollow. The professor wasn't the kind of man to be chased, even if the girl chasing him had made up her mind to marry him. She sighed; probably she would have to rely on Fate, and that lady was notoriously unpredictable. She picked up her tray and bore it back to the kitchen, then crossed the landing to Sister's office. The door stood half open; everyone had gone, Mr Hyde, his firm and his handsome colleague. She might as well get Dora's unfortunate little episode dealt with at once. Undeterred by Sister's cross voice bidding her to go in, she opened the door wider and entered.

Fate at least allowed her to see him again, although the circumstances might have been more propitious; it was quite late in the afternoon when the patient returned to the ward and by then Sister Mack, never the sunniest of persons, was in a quite nasty mood. She had an evening's work before her and instead of being refreshed by a free afternoon, she had been hard at it doing dressings, medicine rounds and writing the beginnings of the day report, while Britannia, as she put it, had been idling in theatre. Britannia hadn't been idling at all, but she knew better than to protest. She had rushed back to the ward while the patient was in the Recovery Room and broken the news to her superior that ICU was up to its neck with a bad car crash and the patient would be coming straight back to his own bed. So she was engrossed in a variety of urgent tasks to do with the wellbeing of the patient when Mr Hyde and the professor arrived at the bedside. They were still in their theatre gear; shapeless white smocks and trousers; the professor, being the size he was, looking as though he might burst every seam although his dignity remained unimpaired. He barely nodded at Britannia before bending over the young man. She handed Mr Hyde the observation sheets she had been keeping, answered his questions with brief clarity, and stood silently until the two men had made their examination. Everything was just as it should be, they told her, she was to continue the treatment which had been ordered—and what, she was asked, were the arrangements for the night?

'There will be a special on at nine o'clock, sir,' said Britannia, and thought longingly of that hour, still some time ahead—tea, and her shoes off and her feet up...

It was disconcerting to her when the professor asked: 'You have been off duty?' because unless he was blind and deaf, which he wasn't, he would have seen her and heard her during the course of the afternoon; indeed, he had stared at her in theatre so intently that she had felt twelve feet tall and outsize to boot.

She handed Mr Hyde her pen so that he could add something to his notes and said composedly: 'No. I can make it up later in the week.'

'No tea?' And when she shook her head: 'A paragon among nurses, Miss Britannia Smith. Let us hope that you will get your just reward.' His voice was bland and the smile she didn't like was back again. She wondered what his real smile was like and wished lovingly that he wasn't quite so difficult. She said a little severely: 'You have no need to turn me into a martyr, Professor. I shall do very well.'

The two surgeons went presently; the professor's casual nod seemed positively churlish compared with Mr Hyde's courteous thanks and genial good evening. Britannia, fiddling expertly with tubes, mused sadly on her day. Surely when one met the man of one's dreams, it should be the happiest day of one's life? If that were so, then hers had fallen sadly short of that.

Sister went to supper at seven o'clock, leaving a student nurse in charge of the ward with the remark that Staff Nurse Smith was there and able to cope with anything which might turn up; she was still bad-tempered at the loss of her off-duty, and the fact that Britannia couldn't leave her patient didn't seem to have struck her, nor did it strike her that Britannia might like her supper too, for when she returned from her meal she finished the report, gave it to the night staff when they came on, and pausing only long enough to tell Britannia that she was worn out with her day's work, hurried off duty. The special wasn't coming on duty for another hour; Britannia, dealing with the dozens of necessary chores for her patient, hardly noticed where that hour went. Fred had been down earlier, he came again now, expressed his satisfaction as to the patient's condition, told Britannia with the casual concern of an old friend that her hair was coming down, and went away.

She still had no time to have done anything to her hair when she at last got off duty. Men's Surgical was on the first floor and she wandered down the staircase to the front hall, listening vaguely to the subdued sounds around her; the faint tinkle of china as the junior night nurses collected up bedtime drinks, the sudden distant wail of some small creature up on the children's unit above her, the creak of trolleys and the muffled to-ing and fro-ing of the night staff. She yawned hugely, gained the last stair and turned, her eyes on the ground, to go down the narrow passage which would take her to the Nurses' Home. She was brought up short by something large and solid—Professor Luitingh van Thien.

'Put on that cloak,' he advised her in a no-nonsense voice. 'We are going out.'

Britannia, aware of the intense pleasure of seeing

him again, opened her mouth, closed it and then opened it again to say: 'I can't—my hair!'

He gave her a considered look. 'A mess. Why do women always worry about their hair? No one is going to look at you.'

She was forced to agree silently and with regret; not that she minded about that but because he didn't consider her worth looking at.

He had taken her hospital cape from her arm and flung it around her shoulders.

'And you have no need to look like that; you are a handsome creature who can manage very well without elaborate hairstyles or other such nonsense.'

She was torn between pleasure at being called a handsome creature—even though it put her strongly in mind of some outsized horse—and annoyance at his casual dismissal of her appearance. 'I don't think I want to go out,' she told him calmly.

'Tea? Hot buttered toast? Sandwiches? Are you not famished?'

Her mouth watered, but: 'I can make myself a pot of tea...'

She could have saved her breath; she was swept across the hall and out into the cold November night and walked briskly down a back lane or two and into Ned's Café, a small, brightly lit place much frequented by the hospital staff in need of a hasty snack or cup of coffee.

Britannia, seated willy-nilly at a small plastic table in the middle of the crowded place, put up a hand to tuck in her hair. 'How did you know about this place?' she enquired, and thought how like a man to choose to sit where everyone could see them, and her with her hair streaming around her head like a witch.

'The Surgical Registrar was kind enough to tell me.'

'Oh—haven't you had your supper either?'

His fine mouth twitched at its corners. 'Er—no.' He lifted a finger and Ned came over, his cheerful, round face beaming.

''Ullo, Staff—'ad a bad day? and I bet they didn't give yer time to eat. What's it ter be? A nice bacon sandwich or a nice bit o' cheese on toast? And a pot of tea?'

Britannia's nose twitched with anticipation. 'Oh, Ned, I'd love a bacon sandwich—and tea, please.'

They both glanced at the professor, who said at once: 'A generous supply of bacon sandwiches, please, and the cheese on toast sounds nice—we'll have that too—and the tea, of course.'

The tea was hot and strong, the bacon sandwiches delicious. Britannia sank her splendid teeth into one of them before asking: 'Why are you buying me my supper, Professor? It's very kind of you, of course, you have no idea how hungry I am—but I'm sur-

prised. You see, I sent you all the way back to the
ward this morning, didn't I, and I haven't apologised
for it yet. I'm sorry, really I am—if you had said
who you were...' She eyed him thoughtfully. 'I expect people mostly know who you are...'

Her companion smiled faintly. 'Mostly.' He
watched her with interest as she daintily wolfed her
sandwich. 'When did you last eat, Miss Smith?'

She licked a finger. 'Well, I should have gone to
second dinner, but Sister was a little late and we had
this emergency in...I had coffee on the ward,
though, and some rice pudding left over from the
patients' dinner.'

The professor looked revolted. 'No wonder you
are hungry!' He pushed the plate towards her. 'It is
nice to see a girl with such a splendid appetite.'

Britannia flushed faintly; she wasn't plump, but
she was a tall girl and magnificently built. Despite
the flush, she gave him a clear, unselfconscious
look. 'There's a lot of me,' she pointed out.

Her companion drank his tea with the air of a man
who was doing his duty and helped himself to one
of the fast disappearing sandwiches. 'You are engaged to be married?' he asked coolly.

'Me? Whatever gave you that idea? No, I'm not.'

'You surprise me. In love, perhaps?'

She flicked a crumb away with the tip of her
tongue. For someone who had known her for a very

short time, his question struck her as inquisitive to say the least. All the same, it didn't enter her head to tell him anything but the truth. 'Yes,' she said briefly, and wondered just what he would say if she told him it was himself.

The toasted cheese had arrived. She poured more tea for them both and sampled the cheese, then paused with her fork half way to her mouth because the professor was looking so very severe. 'It is, of course, only to be expected,' he observed in a nasty smooth voice. 'I suppose I am expected to say what a lucky man he is.'

Britannia munched her cheese; love him she might, but he really was quite disagreeable. 'You aren't expected to say anything,' she pointed out kindly, 'why should you? We hardly know each other and shan't see each other again, so I can't see that it could possibly matter to you. Have another piece of toast before I eat it all.'

The professor curled his lip. 'Thank you, no.' He sat back with his arms folded against his great chest. 'And as to seeing each other again, the unlikelihood of that is something for which I am deeply thankful. I find you far too ready with that sharp tongue of yours.'

Britannia choked on a piece of toast. It was mortifying that the professor should have to get out of his chair and pat her on the back while she spluttered and whooped, but on the other hand it concealed her feelings very satisfactorily. As soon as she could speak she said in a reasonable voice: 'But it is entirely your own fault that you brought me here, you know, unless it was that you wanted to convince yourself of my—my sharp voice.'

She got up suddenly, pulled her cloak around her, thanked him for her supper and made for the door. She was quick on her feet and through it before the professor had a chance to do anything about it— besides, he had to pay the bill. There were several short cuts to the hospital, down small dark alleys which normally she wouldn't have chosen to walk down after dark, but she didn't think about that. She gained the hospital and her room in record time, got ready for bed and then sat down to think. She very much doubted if she would see the professor again, and if she did it would be on the ward where their conversation, if any, would be of the patients. And he had presumably only come for that one case. The thing to do would be to erase him from her mind, something she was loath to do. One didn't meet a man one wanted to marry every day of the week and when one did, the last thing one wanted to do was to forget him. He could have been tired of course, but more probably just a bad-tempered man, given to odd whims. She couldn't for the life of her recall any consultants who had taken staff nurses out for tea and sandwiches at nine o'clock at night, but he looked the kind of man who was accustomed to do as he pleased without anyone attempting to stop him. She got into bed, punched up her pillows and continued to muse, this time on the probability of him being engaged; he wasn't a young man, and surely he would have an attachment of some sort. But if he hadn't... She lay down and closed her eyes; somehow or other she intended to meet him again and some time in the future, marry him. She slept soundly on her resolution.

CHAPTER TWO

THE PROFESSOR came to the ward twice the next day; during the morning when Britannia was scrubbed and doing a lengthy dressing behind screens, so that all she could hear was his deep voice at the other end of the ward. And in the afternoon when he came again, she was at tea.

Sister Mack, giving her the report before she went off duty in the evening, mentioned that he would be leaving for Edinburgh the following day and then returning to Holland. 'A charming man,' she observed, 'although he never quite explained how it was he knew about those tests…' She shot a look at Britannia as she spoke, and Britannia looked placidly back and said nothing at all.

She went about her evening duties rather morosely. She had had no plans concerning the professor, except that she had hoped that if and when they met again something would happen; she had no idea what, but she was a romantic girl as well as a determined one, and without being vain she was aware that she was worth looking at. Of course, it would have been easier if she had been small and blonde and helpless; men, so her brothers frequently told her, liked their women fragile. She looked down at her own splendid person and wished she could be something like Alice and become miraculously fairylike. And David Ross hadn't helped; he had grumbled about his spoilt evening without once showing any sympathy for her own disappointment. They had met as she was on her way to dinner and he had spoken quite sharply, just as though she had done it deliberately, and when she had pointed out reasonably enough that if he wanted to grumble at someone it should have been Mr Hyde, he had shrugged his shoulders and bade her a cool goodbye.

She had had no deep feelings about David, but before the professor had loomed so largely over her world, she had begun to think that given time she might have got around to the idea of marrying him later on. But she was sure that she would never want to do that—indeed, she didn't want to marry anyone else but Professor Luitingh van Thien. She stopped writing the Kardex for a moment and wrote Britannia Luitingh van Thien on the blotting paper; it looked, to say the least, very imposing.

She went home for her days off at the end of the week; she managed to travel down to Dorset at least once a month and although the month wasn't quite up, she felt the urge to talk to her parents. Accordingly she telephoned her mother, packed an overnight bag and caught the evening train, sleeping peacefully until the train came to a brief halt at Moreton station, a small, isolated place, some way from the village of that name and several miles from Dorchester and Wareham. It was cold and dark and Britannia was the only passenger to alight on to the ill-lit platform, but her father was there, passing the time of day with Mr Tims, porter, stationmaster and ticket collector rolled into one. They both greeted her with pleasure and after an animated discussion about Mrs Tims' nasty back and Mr Tims' bunions, they parted, Mr Tims to return to his stuffy little cubbyhole and await the next train and Britannia and Mr Smith to the car outside; an elderly Morris Oxford decidedly vintage and Mr Smith's pride and joy. They accomplished the short journey home without haste, because the country road was winding and very dark and the Oxford couldn't be expected to hurry anyway, and their conversation was casual and undemanding. But once through the front door of the small Georgian cottage which was Britannia's home, they were pounced upon by her mother, a tall older replica of herself who rattled off a succession of questions without waiting for any of them to be answered. Britannia, quite used to this, kissed her parent with deep affection, told her that she looked smashing and remarked on the delicious aroma coming from the kitchen.

'You're famished,' said Mrs Smith immediately. 'I was only saying to your father this evening that you never get proper meals in that hospital.' She started kitchenwards. 'Take off your coat, darling, supper's ready.' She added to no one in particular: 'It will be a blessing when you marry, Britannia.'

Which could mean anything or nothing, thought her daughter as she went upstairs to the small room which had been hers since she was a very small girl. When her brothers had left home her mother had suggested that she might like to move into either of the two bigger rooms they had occupied, but she had chosen to remain in the little room over the porch. She flung her coat down on to the bed now, then went downstairs again without bothering to look in the looking glass; supper for the moment was far more important than her appearance. It was after that satisfying meal, eaten in the cheerful rather shabby dining room opposite the sitting room, when her parents were seated on each side of the fire and she was kneeling before it giving it a good poke, that she paused to look over her shoulder and say: 'I've met the man I want to marry, my dears.'

Her father lifted his eyes from the seed catalogue he was studying and gave her a searching look and her mother cast down her knitting and said encouragingly: 'Yes, dear? Do we know him?'

'No.'

'He's asked you to marry him?'

'No.' Britannia sounded matter-of-fact. 'Nor is he likely to. He's a professor of surgery, one of the best—very good-looking, ill-tempered, arrogant and rich. He didn't like me overmuch. We—we don't come from the same background.'

Her father, longing to get back to his seeds, said vaguely: 'Not at all suitable, I gather.'

It was her mother who asked: 'How old is he, darling? And is he short or tall, fat or thin?'

'It doesn't matter what he looks like if he's unsuitable,' her father pointed out sensibly.

'Quite unsuitable,' agreed Britannia. 'He's in his late thirties, I understand, and he's very large indeed. He's Dutch and he went back to Holland a few days ago.'

'Do we know anyone in Holland?' queried her mother.

Britannia threw her parent a grateful look for taking her seriously. 'No—at least, one of the staff nurses—Joan Stevens, remember her, you met her at the prize-giving—she has a Dutch godmother and she's going over there to stay with her for a couple of weeks very soon. It's a small country,' she added thoughtfully.

'Very. Joan's a good friend of yours?' Her father had left his catalogue to join in the conversation again.

'Oh, yes, Father. We were in the same set, you know, we've known each other for years. She did suggest that I might like to go with her this time.'

'And of course you said yes.'

Britannia nodded and laid the poker down. 'Am I being silly? You see, it was like a sign, if you see what I mean...'

Her parents nodded in complete understanding. 'You've always known what you have wanted,' observed her father, and, 'Have you plenty of pretty clothes?' asked her mother.

She said that yes, she had, and added earnestly: 'I had to do something about it. I'm not sure what, but Joan asking me to go with her seemed like a sign...'

'He'll be a lucky man,' remarked her father, 'if he gets you—though I should have put that the other way round, shouldn't I?' He added: 'It's a pity he's rich—it tends to spoil people.'

His daughter considered this. 'Not him, I think— I fancy he takes it for granted.'

'How did you meet?' her mother wanted to know.

'I sent him packing out of the sluice on Men's Surgical. I didn't know who he was, but he shouldn't have been there, anyway.'

'Hardly a romantic background.' Mr Smith's voice was dry.

'No—well...' Britannia sounded uncertain, for

only a moment. 'Don't say a word to Ted or Nick, will you?'

'Of course not, dear,' promised her mother comfortably. 'Anyway, they're neither of them coming home for weeks. Such dear boys,' she continued, 'and good brothers to you, too, even though they tease.' She picked up her knitting again. 'What's his name?'

'Professor Luitingh van Thien. He's not married, but I daresay he's engaged or got a girl-friend.'

'Quite suitable,' commented her mother, and shot her husband a smug look. 'And one doesn't know, probably he's a misogynist.'

Her husband and daughter surveyed her with deep affection. 'In that case,' declared Mr Smith, 'he won't be suitable at all.'

The first thing Britannia did when she got back to St Jude's was to go in search of her friend. She found her in the pantry, making tea after her day's work, and said without preamble: 'Joan, you asked me if I'd like to go to Holland with you—well, I would, very much.'

Joan warmed the pot carefully. 'Super! The Veskes are dears but a trifle elderly, if you know what I mean. I'm a bit active for them, that's why they suggested that I should bring someone with me. Could you manage two weeks?'

Britannia nodded. 'Mack will be furious, but I haven't had leave for ages—she asked me to change with her, so she owes me a favour. When do you plan to go?'

'Ten days.' They had gone back to Joan's room and were sipping their tea. 'Can you manage that?' And when Britannia nodded again: 'Can you ride?'

'Yes—nothing too mettlesome, though.'

'And cycle? Good. I daresay the weather will be foul, but who cares? We can borrow the car if we want, too. Hoenderloo is fairly central and we could travel round a bit.'

Holland was small, thought Britannia, they would be able to visit a great many places, there was always the chance that she might meet the professor... 'Won't your godmother mind? I mean if we go off all day?'

'Not a bit of it, as long as we're home for dinner in the evening—they like to play cards in the evening—besides, we can always take her with us. She's pretty hot on a bike too.'

'Thick clothes?' asked Britannia.

'And a mac. Not much chance of dressing up, ducky, though I always pop in something pretty just in case Prince Charming should rear his handsome head.' Joan poured more tea. 'And talking of him, what happened to that splendid type who came to operate on that liver case of yours? I saw him in theatre for a minute or two and he quite turned me on.'

'He went back to Holland.' Britannia made her voice nicely vague. 'He made a good job of that liver, too.'

Her friend gave her a considered look. 'Britannia, are you up to something?'

'Me? What could I be up to?'

'Well, you haven't been out with Ross lately, and you were seen wining and dining in Ned's Café.'

'Cheese on toast and a pot of tea,' said Britannia in a very ordinary voice. 'Neither of us had had any food for ages and we happened to meet—he was very rude,' she added.

'So much for Prince Charming,' declared Joan comfortably. 'Oh, well, let's hope he turns up for both of us before we're too long in the tooth.'

It wasn't easy to persuade Sister Mack that she could manage very nicely without her staff nurse for a fortnight, but Britannia's mind had been made up; she was going to Holland, childishly certain that she would meet the professor again. What she would say to him when she did, she had no idea—that could be thought about later. Once having wrung her superior's reluctant consent, she clinched the matter at the office, telephoned her parents and began on the important task of overhauling her wardrobe.

Joan had said something warm and sensible; she

had a Scottish tweed suit she had providentially
bought only a few weeks previously, a rich brown,
the colour of peat, into which had been woven all
the autumn colours of the Scottish Highlands. She
bought a handful of sweaters to go with it, decided
that her last year's brown tweed coat would have to
do, added a small stitched velvet hat which could be
pulled on at any angle and still look smart, and then
a modicum of slacks and thick pullovers before con-
centrating on the important question of something
pretty. For of course when she and the professor did
meet, she would be wearing something eye-catching
and chic... To be on the safe side, she bought two
new dresses, one long, with a sweeping skirt and a
plainly cut bodice. It had long sleeves demurely
cuffed and its soft pink, she felt sure, would enchant
even the cold eye of the professor. The other dress
was short; a dark green wool, elegant and simple
and in its way, equally eye-catching.

The two girls left for their holiday on a cold grey
day which threatened drizzle, and indeed when they
arrived at Schiphol it was raining, a cold, freezing
rain which made them glad that they had worn raincoats and tied scarves over their heads. Mijnheer
Veske was waiting for them, a tall, quiet man whose
English was excellent and whose welcome was sin-
cere. He stowed them into his Citroën and throughout the sixty-mile journey kept up a running com-

mentary on the country they were passing through, but as he travelled fast and the greater part of the journey was a motorway, Britannia at least got a little muddled, but just before Apeldoorn he left the motorway, to take a quiet country road winding through the Veluwe to Hoenderloo, a small town composed largely of charming little villas surrounded by gardens, which even in the winter were a pleasure to the eye. But they didn't stop here, but took a narrow country road lined with tall trees and well wooded on either side, their density broken here and there by gated lanes or imposing pillars guarding well-kept drives.

Presently Mijnheer Veske turned the car into one of the lanes, its gate invitingly opened on to a short gravelled drive leading to a fair-sized house. It was elaborately built, with a great many little turrets and tiled eyebrows over its upstairs windows, and small iron balconies dotted here and there. But it looked welcoming, and indeed when the front door was flung open, their welcome was everything they could have wished for; Mevrouw Veske was waiting for them in the hall, a short, stout lady with carefully coiffured hair, a massive bosom and a round cheerful face. She embraced them in turn, declared herself to be enchanted to entertain her goddaughter's friend, outlined a few of the activities arranged for their entertainment and swept them into a large and cosily furnished sitting room, barely giving them time to shed their outdoor things. The room was warm and a tea tray stood ready; very soon they were all sitting round talking away on the very best of terms.

Presently the two girls were taken upstairs to their rooms, pleasant apartments overlooking the now bare garden at the back and the woods beyond, and left to unpack. Britannia, happily arranging her clothes in a vast, old-fashioned wardrobe, decided that she was going to enjoy herself. It would of course be marvellous if she were to meet the professor, but during their drive from Schiphol she had come to the conclusion that she had been a little mad to imagine that she might find him again. Holland might be small, but not as small as all that. She changed into the new green dress, piled her hair into a great bun above her neck, did her face and went along to see if Joan was ready to go down.

The evening had been very pleasant, she decided, lying in her warm bed some hours later. Dinner had been a substantial meal, taken in a rather sombre dining room and served by a hefty young girl who looked at them rather as though they had arrived from outer space and giggled a good deal. Berthe, explained Mevrouw Veske, was learning to be a general help in the house and doing her best. There was an older woman, it seemed, with the astonishing name of Juffrouw Naakdgeboren, who was away at a family wedding. 'Very important they are, too,' explained their kindly hostess, 'in the country at least it's a very gay affair.' She smiled at them both. 'That's something you have to look forward to, isn't it?'

Britannia had smiled back, agreeing fervently if silently, though whether the professor would fit into a gay affair was something she very much doubted. And really, she reminded herself crossly, she must stop behaving as though she were going to marry him; it was one thing to make plans and hope, quite another to take it for granted. She had the feeling that the professor wouldn't take kindly to being taken for granted.

It was raining when they got up the next morning, but since they were on holiday they had no intention of letting the weather spoil their days. They put on raincoats again, muffled themselves in scarves, thick gloves and high boots and accompanied Mijnheer Veske to the garage, where there was quite a selection of bicycles. Britannia, mounting her rather elderly machine dubiously, almost fell off again because she hadn't realised that its brakes were operated by putting the pedals into reverse, but after a rather hilarious start they pedalled off, down the drive and out into the lane, to take the cycle path running beside the road. Hoenderloo was their destination, and once there they intended to have coffee, buy stamps and have a look round its shops before going back for lunch. Their surroundings, even on a bleak November morning, were pleasant; the bare trees lining the lane formed an arch over their heads, and the woods behind them held every sort of tree.

'Estates,' explained Joan. 'Some of them are quite small, some of them are vast. There are some lovely places tucked away behind these trees, I can tell you, but we shan't get much chance to see many of them—Mevrouw Veske visits here and there, but only the smaller villas. There's a gateway along here, look—something or other rampant on brick pillars and the drive curving away so that we can't see anything at all. It's a castle or moated house or some such thing, I asked Mevrouw Veske last time I was here.'

Britannia was balancing precariously with an eye to the brakes. 'Does anyone live there?' she asked.

'Oh, yes, but I haven't a clue who it is.'

They spent a happy hour or so in Hoenderloo, pottering in and out of its small shops, managing, on the whole, to make themselves understood very well, before having coffee and apple cake and cycling back again. They went with Mevrouw Veske to Apeldoorn in the afternoon, their hostess driving a small Fiat with a good deal of dash and verve and a splendid disregard of speed limits. She took them on a tour of the city's streets, wide and tree-lined and, she assured them, in the summer a mass of colour, and then bustled them back to the town's centre to give them tea and rich cream cakes and drive them home again. They played cards after dinner and went quite late to bed, and on the following day the same pleasant pattern was followed, only this time the girls cycled to the Kroller-Mullermuseum to stare at the van Gogh paintings there, and after lunch Mevrouw Veske took them by car again to Loenen so that they might see the Castle ter Horst, and in the evening they played light-hearted bridge. Britannia, who didn't much care for cards, was glad that neither her host nor her hostess took the game seriously.

It was raining the next morning and Mevrouw Veske was regretfully forced to postpone her plan to take them to Arnhem for the day, so they settled down to writing postcards and then tossed to see who should go to Hoenderloo and post them. Britannia lost and ten minutes later, rather glad of the little outing, she wheeled her bike out of the garage and set off in the wind and the pouring rain. She had reached the gate and was about to turn on to the cycle path when she saw something in the road, small and black and fluttering. A bird, and hurt. She cast the bike down and ran across to pick it up, the wind tearing the scarf from her head so that her hair, tied back loosely, was instantly wet, flapping round her face and getting in her eyes. It was because of that that she didn't hear or see the approaching car, a magnificent Rolls-Royce Camargue, its sober grey coachwork gleaming in the downpour. It stopped within a foot of Britannia and she looked over her shoulder to see Professor Luitingh van Thien get out. She had the bird in her hand and said without preamble: 'I think its wing is broken—what shall I do?'

'Fool,' said the professor with icy forcefulness, 'darting into the road in that thoughtless fashion. I might have squashed you flat, or worse, gone into a skid and damaged the car.' He held out a hand. 'Give me that bird.'

She handed it over, for once unable to think of anything to say. So dreams did come true, after all, but he hardly seemed in the mood to share her pleasure in the fact. She stood, the rain washing over her in a relentless curtain, while he examined the small creature with gentle hands. 'I'll take it with me,' he said finally, and nodded briefly before getting back into his car. Britannia, made of stuff worthy of her name, followed him.

'Do you live near here?' she asked.

'Yes.' He gave her a cold look which froze the words hovering on her tongue, and drove away.

She stood in the road and watched him go. 'I must be mad,' she cried to the sodden landscape around her. 'He's the nastiest man I've ever set eyes on!' She went back to collect her bike and got on to it and rode off towards Hoenderloo. 'But he took the bird,' she reminded herself, 'and he could have wrung its neck.'

She was almost there and the rain had miraculously ceased when he passed her again, going the other way, and a few moments later had turned and slid to a halt beside her so that she felt bound to get off her bicycle.

'The bird's wing has been set; it will be cared for until it is fit to fly again.' He spoke unsmilingly, but she didn't notice that, she looked at him with delight.

'Isn't it incredible?' she declared. 'I mean, meeting like this after the sluice at St Jude's and now you here, almost next door, as it were.'

He looked down his splendid nose. 'I can see nothing incredible about it,' he said repressively. 'It is a coincidence, Britannia, they occur from time to time.'

He could call it that if he liked. She thought secretly of good fairies and kindly Fate and smiled widely. 'Well, you don't need to be so cross about it. I've never met such a prickly man. Have you been crossed in love or something?'

The ferocious expression which passed over the professor's handsome features might have daunted anyone of lesser spirit than hers. 'You abominable girl!' he ground out savagely. 'I have never met anyone like you...'

Britannia lifted a hand to tuck back a wet strand of hair. 'What you need,' she told him kindly, 'is a wife and a family.'

His mouth quivered momentarily. 'Why?'

She answered him seriously. 'Well, you would have them to look after and care for and love, and they'd love you and bring you your slippers in the evening, and...'

His voice was a well-controlled explosion. 'For God's sake, girl,' he roared, 'be quiet! Of all the sickly sentimental ideas...!'

Two tears welled up in Britannia's fine eyes and rolled slowly down her cheeks. The professor muttered strongly in his own language, and with the air of a man goaded beyond endurance, got out of his car.

'Why are you crying? I suppose that you will tell me that it's my fault.'

Britannia gave a sniff, wiped her eyes on a delicate scrap of white lawn and then blew her nose. 'No, of course it's not your fault, because you can't help it, can you? It's just very sad that you should think of a wife and children as being nothing more than s-sickly s-sentiment.' Two more tears spilled over and she wiped them away impatiently as a child would, with the back of her hand.

The professor was standing very close to her. When he spoke it was with surprising gentleness. 'I didn't mean that. I was angry.'

She said in a woeful voice, 'But you're always losing your temper—every time we meet you rage and roar at me.'

'I neither rage nor roar, Britannia. Possibly I am a little ill-tempered at times.' The gentleness had a decidedly chilly edge to it now.

'Oh, yes, you do,' she answered him with spirit. 'You terrify me.' She peeped at him, to see him frowning.

'I cannot believe that you are terrified of anyone or anything, certainly not of me. Try that on some other man, my dear girl, I'm not a fool.'

She sighed. 'Well, no—I was afraid you wouldn't believe me.'

He looked at her with cold interest. 'And were the tears a try-out too?'

She shook her head slowly; she might have met him again, just as she had dreamed that she might, but it hadn't done much good. She said quietly: 'Thank you very much for taking care of the bird,' and got on to her bike and wobbled off at a great rate, leaving him standing there.

She tried very hard not to think of him during the rest of the day, but lying in bed was a different matter; she went over their meetings, not forgetting a word or a look, and came to the conclusion that he still didn't like her. She was on the point of sleep when she remembered with real regret that she had hardly looked her best; surely, if she had been wearing the new pink dress, he would have behaved differently? Men, her mother had always said, were susceptible to pink. Britannia sighed and slept.

CHAPTER THREE

IT SEEMED THAT Britannia was never to discover the professor's taste regarding pink-clad females, but that was a small price to pay in the face of the frequency of their meetings. For she met him again the very next afternoon. Joan, laid low with a headache, had decided to stay indoors and Mevrouw Veske had an appointment with her dentist. Britannia, restless and urged by her friend to take advantage of the unexpectedly pleasant day, donned slacks, pulled on two sweaters, tied a scarf under her chin and went to fetch her bicycle. There was miles of open country around her; she chose a right-hand turn at the crossroads and pedalled down it, feeling a good deal more cheerful while she plotted ways and means—most of them quite unsuitable—of meeting the professor again. An unnecessary exercise as it turned out, for seeing a picturesque pond among the trees on the other side of the road she decided to cross over and get a better view. She was almost there when the professor's magnificent car swept round the curve ahead and stopped within a foot or so of her.

She jumped off her machine, quite undisturbed by

the sight of his furious face thrust through the open
window, and his biting: 'This is becoming quite ri-
diculous—you're not fit to ride a bicycle!'

Britannia, a girl of common sense, nonetheless
realised that her fairy godmother, kind Fate or just
plain good luck were giving her another chance. The
sight of the professor glowering from the opened
window of his stupendous car sent a most pleasing
sensation through her, although her pretty face remained calm. She said: 'Hullo,' and got no reply;
the professor was swallowing rage. When he did at
length speak, his voice was cold and nasty.

'You were on the wrong side of the road. I might
have killed you.'

She stooped to pick up her bicycle, observing that
it had a puncture in the back tyre which seemed of
no great importance at the moment; it was much
more important to get him into a good mood. She
said reasonably: 'I'm a foreigner, so you have to
make allowances, you know. You aren't very nice
about it; after all, we have met before.'

The blue eyes studied her in undisguised rage.
'Indeed we have, but I see no reason to express pleasure at seeing you again. I advise you to travel on
the correct side of the road and use the cycle path
where there is one.' He added morosely: 'You're not
fit to be out on your own.'

Britannia took his criticism in good part. 'You can

come with me if you like,' she invited. 'I daresay
some healthy exercise would do you good; there's
nothing like fresh air to blow away bad temper.' She
smiled at him kindly and waited for him to speak,
and when he didn't she went on: 'Oh, well, perhaps
you can't cycle any more...'

The professor's voice, usually deep and measured,
took on an unexpected volume. 'You are an atrocious girl. How you got here and why is no concern
of mine, but I will not be plagued by you.'

She looked meek. 'I don't mean to plague you.
My back tyre's punctured.'

'Mend it or walk home!' he bellowed, and left
her standing there.

'He drives much too fast,' remarked Britannia to
the quiet road. 'And how do I mend a puncture with
nothing?'

She turned her machine and started to walk, doing
sums as she went. She had been cycling for almost
an hour—not hurrying—so she must have come at
least ten miles. She would be late for lunch, she
might even be late for tea. She had passed through
a village some way back, but as she had no money
and no one there would know or understand her, it
wouldn't be of much use to stop there. She had been
walking for twenty minutes or so when an elderly
man on a bicycle passed her, stopped, and with the
minimum of speech and fuss, got out his repair kit.

He had almost finished the job when the professor, coming the other way, slid his car to a halt beside them.

Britannia gave him a warm smile. 'There, I knew you weren't as nasty as you pretended you were!'

He surveyed her unsmilingly. 'Get in,' he said evenly. 'The bike can be fetched later.'

She shook her head at him. 'Oh, I couldn't do that; this gentleman stopped to help me and I wouldn't be so ungrateful as to leave him now.' She shook her pretty head at him again. 'You really must get out of the habit of expecting people to do what you want whether they wish to or not. This kind man hasn't shouted at me, nor did he leave me to mend a puncture all alone in a strange land, which I couldn't have done anyway because I had nothing to do it with.'

She paused to see the effect of this speech. The professor's splendid features appeared to be carved in disapproving stone, his eyes pale and hard. She sighed. 'Oh, well...it was kind of you to come back. Thank you.' She had no chance to say more, for he had gone, driving much too fast again.

She very nearly told Joan about it when she got back, but really there didn't seem much point; beyond meeting the professor again, nothing had happened; he still disliked her, indeed, even more so, she thought. There was the possibility that she might not see him again. She paused in the brushing of her mane of hair to reflect that whether he liked her or no, they had met again—she could have stayed her whole two weeks in Holland and not seen hair nor hide of him; she tended to regard that as some sort of sign. Before she got into bed she sat down and wrote to her mother and father; after all, she had told them about him in the first place, they had a right to know that her sudden whim to go to Holland had borne fruit. Rather sour fruit, she conceded.

But not as sour as all that; she was on her way down to breakfast the following morning when Berthe came running upstairs to meet her. She pointed downwards, giggling, and then pointed at Britannia, who instantly thought of all the awful things which could have happened to either Mijnheer or Mevrouw Veske and rushed past her and down the stairs at a great rate.

'I had no idea that you were so eager to see me again,' said the professor. 'Should I be flattered?'

He was standing in the hall, in his car coat with his gloves in his hand, and gave her the distinct impression that he was impatient to be gone.

'No,' said Britannia, 'you shouldn't—I thought something awful had happened to the Veskes. What are you doing here? Is someone ill?'

The professor's lip twitched faintly. 'Cut down to size,' he murmured. 'I called to see you.'

Britannia's incurable optimism bubbled up under her angora sweater, but she checked it with a firm metaphorical hand and asked: 'Why?'

'I owe you an apology for my behaviour yesterday. I offer it now.'

'Well, that's handsome of you, Professor, I'll accept it. I expect you were worrying about something and felt irritable.'

'You concern yourself a little too much about my feelings, Miss Smith. Perhaps it would be better if you were to attend to your own affairs.'

She had annoyed him again. The optimism burst its bubble and she said quietly: 'I'm sure you're right. Thank you for coming—I expect you want to go...'

He gave her a long look and went to the door without a word, but before he could open it she had nipped across the hall to stand beside him. 'I'm only here for a fortnight,' she told him, and then, unable to resist the question: 'Do you really live near here?'

'Yes. Goodbye, Britannia.'

So that was that. She went into breakfast and made lighthearted rejoinders to the questions fired at her, and presently they all began talking about their plans for the day and the professor was forgotten.

They spent the next day or so sightseeing; Mevrouw Veske was a splendid hostess. They drove to

Arnhem and spent several hours in the Open-Air Museum, absorbing Holland's national culture through centuries through its farms, windmills, houses from every province and medieval crafts, and were taken to lunch at the Haarhuis, where Britannia ate eel, so deliciously disguised that she had no idea what it was until her hostess told her. They spent the afternoon looking at the shops and buying a few trifles to take home, and arrived back at the villa exhausted but very content with their day.

The next day was Saturday and Mijnheer Veske had offered to take the two girls riding. The weather had turned cold and bright and he knew the charming country around them like the back of his hand. Britannia, a rather wary horsewoman, found that she was enjoying herself immensely; her mount was a calm beast who made no effort to play tricks but was content to trot along after the other two, so that Britannia relaxed presently and looked around her. There were woods on either side of them, with here and there a small estate between the trees. Mijnheer Veske, who had lived there all his life, found nothing out of the ordinary about it, but she longed to explore away from the lanes; the glimpses of the houses she saw fired her imagination, and just as they were about to return home she caught a glimpse of a really splendid house, its gables tantalisingly half hidden by the trees surrounding it. There was a narrow lane running round the walls of the grounds, too. It was on the tip of her tongue to ask her host if they might ride a little way along so that she might see more of it, but it was already eleven o'clock and she knew that the Veskes lunched at midday. She made herself a promise that before she went back to England she would either cycle or ride that way and see it for herself.

They all went to church the next morning, driving to Hoenderloo in the Citroën. Britannia couldn't help but wonder if the service would be of any benefit to herself and Joan, but it had been taken for granted that they would accompany the Veskes, and it would be an experience.

The church was red brick, built in the jelly-mould style with whitewashed walls and plain glass windows. It was lofty and spacious and on the cold side, but Britannia forgot all about that in her interest in following the service. It seemed one stood up when one would kneel at home, and sat down when one would stand, but the hymns, surprisingly, had the same tunes even though the words were incomprehensible. They were sung rather slowly too, so that she had the chance to try out some of the verses, much to Joan's amusement. It was as the sermon began that she saw the professor, sitting in the front of the church and to her right, and he wasn't alone. Beside him was a fair-haired girl with a beanpole figure draped in the height of fashion. Britannia, sitting between her host and hostess, wondered about her. She was undeniably beautiful if one liked glossy magazine types. She glanced down at her own nicely rounded person and sighed to be slim and golden-haired. There was only one tiny crumb of comfort; the professor didn't look at his companion once; his arrogant profile was lifted towards the *dominee*, thundering away at the congregation from under his sounding-board.

And presently, as the congregation left the church, the professor and his companion passed the Veskes' pew. He acknowledged their greeting pleasantly, smiled nicely at Joan and then wiped the smile off his face as he bent his cold eyes on Britannia, who so far forgot herself as to wrinkle her nose at him and turn down the corners of her pretty mouth in an unladylike grimace. If he wanted war, he should have it!

A belligerent decision which was made to look silly, for as they rose from Sunday lunch the professor arrived at the front door to enquire for her, and when she went into the sitting room where the giggling Berthe had shown him, it was to find him nattily attired in tweeds and an anorak, with the bland invitation to go cycling with him.

'Me?' asked Britannia, much astonished.

He opened his eyes wide in exaggerated surprise.

'Certainly you. I was under the impression that you had asked me to accompany you—healthy exercise, you said, and the certainty that fresh air would be good for my temper.'

She eyed him with astonishment. 'And you've actually got a bike? You want to go cycling? With me?'

'Yes.'

She beamed at him; the fairies were very much on her side after all. 'Give me two minutes,' she begged him.

It took her rather less than that to pull another sweater over her skirt, wind a scarf round her neck and tie a scarf round her hair, and another minute to explain to Mevrouw Veske, who looked pleased if surprised. 'Well, at least one of us has found Prince Charming,' observed Joan.

'Stuff!' retorted Britannia. 'He's only doing it because he thinks I'm a fool on a bike.'

'Well, you are, ducky,' said Joan cheerfully. 'I expect he'll teach you the rules of the road.'

But he didn't; they cycled amiably enough along the route she had chosen and when he asked why she particularly wanted to go that way she told him about the house she had glimpsed and hadn't had time to see. 'It looked exciting, like things do look when you can't see them properly—just the gables between the trees and a lovely park.' She turned to look at him and wobbled alarmingly so that he put out a hand to steady her handlebars. 'I still don't know where you live, you know, and I quite understand that you don't want me to know, though I can't think why, but you must have a house somewhere within cycling distance; you'll know who the house belongs to, I expect. There's a little lane running round the park walls. Do you suppose the owner would mind very much if we went down it and looked over the wall?'

She was so intent on riding her bicycle in a manner to win his approval that she didn't see the professor's expression. Astonishment, amusement and then sheer delight passed over his features, but none of these were apparent in his voice. 'I believe it is possible to cycle right round the grounds—there should be a better view of the house. Why are you so interested?'

'Well, it sounds silly, but I had a funny feeling when I saw it first—as though it meant something to me.' She glanced at him and found him smiling and went on defensively, 'All right, so it's silly— I'm not even in my own country and I don't know anyone here except the Veskes—and you. Perhaps it's derelict.'

Her companion looked shocked. 'No—someone lives in it.'

'Oh, you know them?'

'Yes.'

They had passed the crossroads and were in the narrow lane curving between the trees with the professor leading the way.

'What I like about you,' observed Britannia, 'is the terseness of your answers.'

He slowed a little so that she could catch up with him. 'I had no idea that there was anything you liked about me,' he said suavely.

Which annoyed her so much that she forgot about the brakes and back-pedalled so that he had to put a steadying hand on her arm. 'Now, now,' he chided her in a patient, superior voice which annoyed her even more.

But she couldn't remain vexed for long; the air was cold and exhilarating and the countryside charming, and had she not got just what she had wished for most? The professor's company...

'It's down here,' she said eagerly, 'if we go along here and look to the left...'

'There will be a better view further on,' observed the professor matter-of-factly.

'Why are you laughing?' asked Britannia.

'My dear good girl, I am not even smiling.'

'Inside you—something's amusing you...'

He shot her a quick look. 'I can see that I shall have to be very careful of my behaviour when we are together,' he said smoothly. 'Since you asked, I was remembering something which amused me.'

She let that pass, although it was nice, she reflected, that the professor could be amused... 'There!' she exclaimed, and back-pedalled to a halt. 'That's the place. It must be sheer heaven in the summer—all those copper beeches and that row of limes. I wonder what the garden is like.'

'Probably if we go on a little further we could see it,' suggested her companion. He was right; the house came into view, typically Dutch, of mellow red brick, tall chimneypots among the gables, its large windows shining in the pale sunshine. It was too far off to see as much as she wanted, but she could glimpse a paved walk all round the house, outbuildings at the side of a formal garden laid out before its massive front.

'I hope whoever lives there loves it,' remarked Britannia. 'Do you suppose it belongs to some old family? Perhaps it had to be sold to pay death duties and now there's someone living there who can't tell Biedermeier from mid-Victorian Rococo...'

'What a vivid imagination you have! And do you really know the difference between Rococo and Biedermeier?' He wasn't looking at her but staring across the countryside towards the distant house.

'Yes, I think so. You see, my father is an antique

dealer and I always went with him to sales and auctions. I didn't mean to boast.'

'You admire antique furniture? Which is your favourite period?'

Britannia had got off her bike and was leaning against the low wall. 'Oh, yes. Early Regency and Gothic.'

He asked casually, 'Have you been inside any of the houses round here?'

She shook her head. 'No, and I don't expect to. I only came to keep Joan company—she's the Veskes' goddaughter.' She got on her bike again. 'Can we get all the way round, or do we go back the way we came?'

The professor smiled faintly. 'You wish to return? We can go on. Do you intend visiting any of the hospitals while you are here?'

'I'd like to, but one can't just present oneself and say look, I'm a nurse, can I look round. Mijnheer Veske might be able to give me an introduction, but Joan isn't keen, anyway.'

They were side by side, pedalling into the chilly wind. 'I should be glad to arrange a visit for you,' said the professor surprisingly. 'Arnhem—I go there twice a week. I will call for you and bring you back after my teaching round.'

Britannia eyed him with surprise. 'Would you really? Why are you being so nice? I thought you couldn't bear the sight of me.'

His voice was smooth. 'Shall we say that the fresh air and exercise which you recommended have had their good effect?'

He didn't go into the house with her but bade her a casual goodbye without saying another word about her visit to the hospital. Probably he had regretted his words, decided Britannia as she went to her room to tidy herself before presenting herself in the sitting room for tea.

There were visitors; an elderly couple, their daughter and a son, home from some far-flung spot on long leave. Britannia was made instantly aware of the interesting fact that he and Joan were getting on remarkably well and being a true friend, engaged the daughter in a conversation which lasted until the visitors got up to leave.

Their car had barely disappeared down the drive when Joan told her happily: 'We're going out to-morrow. Britannia, do you mind? I mean, if you're left on your own. He's only got another week...'

'Plenty of time,' comforted Britannia. 'Besides, it was an instant thing, wasn't it? Flashing lights and sunbeams and things, it stuck out a mile.' She added: 'Prince Charming, love?'

Joan looked smug and hopeful and apprehensive

all at the same time. 'Oh, yes. Oh, Britannia, you've no idea how it feels!'

In which she was wrong, of course.

Britannia, happily, did not have long to wait before the professor paid her another visit, although visit was hardly the right word. He drove up some time after breakfast, asked to see her, and when she presented herself, enquired of her coolly if she was ready to go to Arnhem with him. She felt a surge of pleasure, for Joan was committed for the whole day with Dirk de Jonge and Mevrouw Veske had asked her a little anxiously what she was going to do with herself until lunchtime; all the same she said sedately: 'How kind, but I didn't know that you had asked me to come with you today. It's not very convenient…'

He stood bareheaded in the hall, watching her. 'May I ask what you intended doing today?' His voice was very bland.

'Nothing,' said Britannia before she could stop herself, and then waited for him to make some nasty remark. But he didn't, he said quite mildly: 'In that case I should be glad to take you to Arnhem. I think you will find the hospital interesting. You have, after all, nearly a week here, have you not, and if your friend is going to spend it exclusively with de Jonge you will have to seek your own amusement, will you not?'

'Do you know him? I thought he looked nice...'

'Yes, I know him, and if by nice you mean unmarried, able to support a wife and anxious to marry your friend, then yes, he is nice.'

'You have no need to talk like that. You must live close by...?'

His brief 'Yes,' didn't help at all. Britannia sighed. 'I'll fetch my coat.'

Mevrouw Veske gave her a roguish look when she disclosed her plans for the day. 'Very nice, dear, I'm sure you'll enjoy yourself, and in such good company too.' She wore the pleased expression that older ladies wore when they scented romance with a capital R, and Britannia, incurably honest, made haste to explain that she was merely being given a lift to the hospital and a return lift when it was convenient to the professor. Rather a waste of time, for Mevrouw Veske, accompanying her to the hall to bid the professor good morning, wished them both a pleasant day together, with an arch look which wasn't lost on him, for the moment they were in the car he remarked silkily:

'Your hostess seems to be under the impression that we are to spend the day in each other's company. I hope that you don't think the same.'

'No,' said Britannia sweetly, and seethed silently as she said it, 'I don't—but you know what happily married women are like, they want to see everyone else happily married; such an absurd notion in our case that I see no point in wasting breath on it.'

'Why absurd?' he asked blandly.

Britannia settled down comfortably in her seat. 'Well,' she explained carefully, 'we're in—incompatible, aren't we? Different backgrounds and interests and…and…'

'Ages?' he queried.

'Lord no—what has age got to do with it? That was a very pretty girl in church with you.'

'Yes.'

'Does she live close by, too?'

'Yes.'

Britannia turned to look at him. 'I wonder why you offered me a lift? Certainly not for the conversation.'

He said blandly: 'I thought I had explained about the fresh air and exercise…'

'Oh, pooh. I shall hold my tongue, since you like it that way.'

He ignored this. 'When you get to the hospital you will be put in the care of a surgical Sister who speaks excellent English. She will take you to any wards you wish to see. I shall be a couple of hours— you will be warned when I am ready to leave.'

'Who looks after you?' asked Britannia.

'I have an excellent housekeeper.'

'She must be a devoted one too if you fire orders

at her in the same way as you're firing them at me. You know, I don't think I want to go to Arnhem after all. Would you stop, please? I'll go for a walk instead.'

He laughed aloud. 'We have come almost six miles and this isn't a main road, nor are there any villages—you may have noticed that we are passing the Air Force field. You could walk back the way we have come or continue on to Arnhem. It will be a long...' He broke off and slowed the car's quiet rush. There was a woman standing in the middle of the road, waving her arms and shouting. As the professor brought the car to a halt she ran towards it, still shouting and crying too, and he got out without more ado to catch her by the shoulders and say something firmly to her. Britannia had got out as well, for plainly there was something very wrong. The woman was pointing now, towards a very small, rather tumbledown cottage half hidden in the trees, and the professor started towards it, the woman tugging at his sleeve. 'A child taken ill,' he said briefly, and Britannia went too; after all, she was a nurse and there might be something she could do.

The child was on the floor of the small room, crowded with furniture, into which they went. A little girl, whose small face was already blue and who had no trace of breath. The professor went down on his knees, asking brief, curt questions of the hysterical mother, then turned to Britannia.

'Sit down,' he commanded her. 'Take the child on your knees and flex her head. There's a pebble impacted in her larynx, so her mother says.'

He waited a few seconds while Britannia did as she was bid and then swept an exploratory finger into the child's mouth. 'Have you a Biro pen with you?' he asked, and took a penknife from his pocket.

She didn't say more than she had to, for talk at that time was wasting precious seconds. 'My bag— outside pocket.'

She watched while he found the pen, pulled it apart and handed her the plastic casing; a makeshift trachy tube indeed, but better than nothing.

'Hold the child's head back, give me the tube when I say so,' said the professor, and opened his knife. 'This may just work,' he observed. It took seconds and with the improvised tube in place the little girl's face began to take on a faint pink as air reached her lungs once more. But the professor wasted no time in contemplating his handiwork. 'Get into the car,' he said, and took the child from Britannia's knee and followed her as she ran back to the Rolls. 'Hold her steady on your knee and hold the tube exactly as it is now. I'm going to drive to the hospital.'

Britannia paled a little, but her 'yes,' was said in

a steady enough voice and the professor, acknowledging it with a grunt, went back for the mother, and when she was in the car, still crying and hysterical, picked up the telephone she had noticed beside his seat. He spoke briefly, bent over the child for a moment, got into his seat and drove off smoothly. He drove very fast too; Britannia, her hand locked on the frail plastic tube, sent up a stream of incoherent prayers, mingled with heartfelt thanks that Arnhem couldn't be very far away now. And at the professor's speed, it wasn't. The city's pleasant outskirts enclosed them, gave way to busy streets and in no time at all, the forecourt of a hospital.

His few terse words into the telephone had borne fruit. Two white-coated young doctors, a rather fierce-looking Sister and her attendant satellite were waiting for them. In no time at all the professor was out of the car, round its elegant bonnet and bending over the child through Britannia's open door, with the two young men squeezed in on her other side and the Sister right behind the professor, a covered tray in her hands. He used the instruments on it with lightning speed; the plastic Biro case was eased out and a tracheotomy tube inserted and its tapes neatly tied. The professor muttered and the two doctors immediately started the sucker they had brought with them; after a few moments the child's face began to

look almost normal again while the trachy tube
made reassuring whistling noises with each breath.
The professor spoke again and lifted the child off
Britannia's knee; seconds later she was alone,
stretching her cramped back and legs and watching
the small urgent procession of trolley, professor and
his assistants disappearing into the hospital.

It was almost an hour before anyone came—a
porter, who eyed her with some surprise as he got
into the driver's seat beside her. She bade him a
quite inadequate hullo and hoped that he could
speak English. He could after a fashion, but his 'In
garage' hardly reassured her.

With the British belief that if she spoke enough
he would understand her, Britannia asked: 'Will the
professor be long?' and then when she saw how
hopeless it was, managed a: *'De Professor komt?'*

He shook his head, thought deeply and came out
with: 'Long time.'

He had forgotten her, of course. She smiled at the
man, got out of the car and watched it being driven
away, round to the back of the hospital. She could
go and enquire, she supposed; ask someone where
the professor was and how long he would be, but
she fancied that he wouldn't take kindly to being
disturbed at his work. She walked slowly out of the
hospital gates and started towards the main streets
of the town they had gone through. Sooner or later

she would see a policeman who would tell her where she could get a bus.

It took a little while, for the streets confused her and there seemed to be no policemen at all, but she found one at last, got him to understand what she wanted and set off once more, her head whirling with lengthy instructions as to how and where to get a bus for Hoenderloo, so it was some time later when she boarded the vehicle and wedged herself thankfully between a stout woman and a very thin old man. There would be a mile or so to walk from the bus stop and the afternoon was closing in rapidly, reminding her that she had had no lunch, but she cheered herself up with the thought of the cosy sitting room at the villa and the plentiful dinner Mevrouw Veske set before her guests each evening.

The bus made slow progress, stopping apparently wherever it was most convenient for its passengers to alight, but it reached her stop at last, and she got out quickly, the only passenger to do so, anxious to get back to the villa. She had taken a bare half dozen steps when she saw the professor looming at the side of the road just ahead of her, the Rolls behind him. He took her arm without a word and marched her to the car, declaring coldly: 'You tiresome girl, as though I don't have enough to do without trapesing round the country looking for you!'

She couldn't see his face very clearly in the early

dusk. 'I'm quite able to look after myself,' she pointed out reasonably. 'I didn't know what to do when the porter came to take the car away; he said you would be a long time and I thought that perhaps you intended remaining at the hospital. Is the child all right?'

'Yes.' He gave her arm a little shake. 'You imagined that I would do that without sending you a message? Don't be absurd!'

They were in the car now and she turned to look at him and observe in a kindly tone: 'Not absurd, you know. You had enough to think of without bothering your head about me.' She smiled at him. 'I can't think why you should.'

'I'll tell you why,' he ground out, and then in his usual cool voice: 'But not now.' He started the car without another word.

The Veskes had been very nice about it, Britannia decided as she got ready for bed that evening; they had asked the professor in for a drink, expressing discreet sympathy with her, murmuring comfortably about difficulties with language and misunderstandings. He had stayed for half an hour making polished conversation before making his farewells, not that he had bothered overmuch with his goodbyes to her; a nod, a casual *tot ziens* and her thanks shrugged off carelessly. And come to think of it, he hadn't bothered to thank her for the part she had played that morning. She tugged the covers up to her chin on a wave of indignation. He was arrogant and ill-tempered and just about the horridest man she had ever met, and she loved him with all her heart. All the same, she would cut him dead when she saw him again. She began to concoct episodes in which he was made to appear in a very poor light while she ignored him coolly, but presently she got a little muddled and before she could sort out the muddle, was asleep.

CHAPTER FOUR

THE PROFESSOR called the next afternoon and Britannia quite forgot to be cool and ignore him. Joan had gone off for the day directly after breakfast and now, after a morning shopping with Mevrouw Veske and a lunch à deux, she had got into slacks, a thick sweater and an old anorak of her hostess's and was on her way to fetch her bike. The weather was hardly promising, but Britannia was in no mood to bother about that; she was wondering how she could find out where the professor lived and if possible, despite her determination to ignore him, see him again, so that the sight of him striding towards her round the corner of the house sent her spirits soaring. She stood outside the garage, holding the bike, watching him coming towards her. Beautifully turned out, as always, assured, far too good-looking... She wished him a quiet good afternoon, and waited.

'I thought we might try again,' he said.

The urge to fling her machine to the ground and accept on the instant was very great. She clutched the handlebars with woolly gloved hands and said politely: 'How kind of you. But as you see, I'm just off for a ride.'

He didn't bother to answer her but took the bike from her, leaned it against the garage wall and took her arm. 'It's too cold to cycle. I've warned Zuster Vinke that you would be coming.'

Britannia stopped in her tracks to face him. 'That was a little high-handed of you,' she pointed out.

He grinned. 'I am high-handed, I shout, I'm nasty, ill-tempered, irritable…I forget the rest, although you have told me often enough.' He gave her a little shake. 'I have never been preached at so often in my life before.'

Britannia raised large, serious brown eyes to his. 'Oh, I don't mean to, really I don't; you're a splendid surgeon…'

'And so are thousands of others. Britannia, I'm sorry about yesterday. I was angry because I didn't know where you were, and I was angry with myself for not having done something about it. Forgive me and come with me now.'

'Well, I'm not dressed…' she began, already half won over.

'You look just the same as usual,' he assured her, and even while she was trying to decide if that was a compliment or not, he had her by the arm, walking her briskly along the drive to the waiting car.

There was nothing to interrupt their journey to

Arnhem this time and the professor whiled away the short journey in light conversation, revealing a new facet of himself to Britannia. She had had no idea that he could be such an amusing and pleasant companion; it wouldn't last, of course; sooner or later he would get into a fine rage about something or other. It was extraordinary, she mused, that one could love someone so much even when they scowled and frowned and stared down with cold blue eyes...

'I was saying,' said her companion with exaggerated patience, 'that I hope to be finished by four o'clock. Zuster Vinke will be told when I am ready.'

Such arrogance, she thought lovingly, but she could alter that. Her 'Very well,' was meek.

Zuster Vinke turned out to be a big bony woman, with shrewd eyes behind thick glasses and a nice smile. And her English was more than adequate; she led Britannia from one ward to the next, finishing in the Children's Ward where Britannia was shown the small girl the professor had saved. She was sitting up in bed, playing quite happily with a doll. The pebble had been removed, she was told; as soon as the tracheotomy had healed the child would go to a convalescent home and then back to the isolated little cottage which was her home. It was while they were with her that they were joined by one of the doctors who had met them outside the hospital.

Young and tall and nice-looking, he introduced himself as Tom van Essent. 'And of course I know who you are,' he told her eagerly. 'You were a great help to the professor, so he tells us; without your help the child would have died. It is a pleasure to meet you. You are staying long in Holland?'

'Under a week—not long enough.' Britannia smiled at him, quite ready to like him because he worked for the professor.

'Perhaps if you are not too occupied, I might take you out to dinner one evening?'

'Well, that would be nice, thank you, I'd like that. Could you telephone me some time?' She gave him Mevrouw Veske's number and then, because Zuster Vinke had been called to the telephone and came back with the news that the professor would be ready in five minutes, she went with him back to the entrance hall, with Zuster Vinke striding along on her other side. They were standing together, laughing and talking, when they were joined by the professor, who, making no effort to make a cheerful fourth, bade her two guides a curt goodbye, asked her grumpily if she was ready to leave, and walked out of the hospital at a great rate, with Britannia having to nip along smartly to keep up. In the car, sliding smoothly away from the hospital, he asked: 'You found your visit interesting? I see that young van Essent was with you.' It was coolly and carelessly said, but she thought she detected annoyance as well.

'Oh, he met us just before we returned to the entrance—in the Children's Ward—and he walked down with us. I liked Zuster Vinke and it's a splendid hospital. And how nice to see little Tinneke sitting up playing with a doll.' She turned to look at him. 'Doesn't it give you a nice feeling each time you see her?'

He shot the Rolls through a knot of traffic. His voice was bland. 'Perhaps I haven't your youthful enthusiasm, Britannia.'

'Oh, stuff, of course you have, otherwise you wouldn't be a surgeon, you'd retire to your villa or whatever and mope and moulder away the rest of your days.'

A reluctant smile tugged at the corners of his mouth. 'Put like that I must admit your argument is a strong one. You liked van Essent?'

'Oh yes. He's young, though.'

'And what do you mean by that?'

'Just what I said—he made me think of my younger brother.'

'Ah—so you have brothers. And a sister perhaps?'

'No, only my brothers.'

'And parents?'

'Yes.' Really, he asked a lot of questions! 'And what about you…?'

'I am touched by your interest in me, but there is nothing of interest to tell you.'

'Unfair,' snapped Britannia. 'If you ask me any more questions I shall invent the answers.'

'And I shall know if you are fibbing, Britannia. Did Zuster Vinke give you tea?'

'No—at least she said we would have a cup of coffee when we had finished looking round, but there wasn't time—you sent a message.'

'Thoughtless of me.' They were clear of the town now, racing along the quiet road, passing the cottage where Tinneke lived and then the airfield; they would be at the villa in no time at all. But at the crossroads, instead of keeping straight on, the professor turned down the road Mijnheer Veske had taken when they had gone horse-riding.

'You're going the wrong way,' observed Britannia helpfully.

'I am going to my house. So that you may have that cup of coffee I so thoughtlessly deprived you of.' He slowed the car to turn between two stone pillars. 'Or tea, perhaps—you English drink gallons of tea.'

'That's why we're such nice people. I'd love to see your house.'

'So you have already said.' He didn't sound very

enthusiastic, but she didn't care; she was going to
have her wish after all, and he had been almost
friendly... 'This is someone's park,' she pointed out.
'Should we be here?'

'Of course. It belongs to me.'

She hadn't thought of that; she peered out of the
window, silent for once, her tongue held by surprise.
The sanded drive wound through trees, swept round
a high grass bank and then, with close-cut lawns on
either side of it, made for the house. It was a grey,
dull afternoon and would soon be dark, but Britannia
could see it clearly enough; its gables and chimneys
now wholly visible. And it was just as beautiful as
she had imagined it to be when she had first
glimpsed it from the other side of the park wall. It
wasn't so very large as large houses go, but its windows were wide and high, giving a hint of the spacious rooms within, and although its front was flat,
the windows arranged in neat rows on either side
and above its imposing entrance, there were wings
on either side, red brick and one storey high. There
were trees grouped behind it and great sweeps of
lawn on either side, and a little formal garden just
visible beyond, a miniature of the large one in front
of the house.

'Well,' said Britannia at length, 'you might have
told me.'

'I can see no possible reason for doing so.'

'But I took you to see it the other day…you were there by the wall, you told me there was a better view…'

'I still can see no reason for telling you.' He added silkily: 'In any case, you being you, you would have discovered it for yourself.'

'Yes, of course I should, because I very much wanted to know who lived here. But it wasn't very nice of you—you've made me feel like a busybody poking her nose into other people's business.'

'If I thought that I shouldn't be bringing you here for tea, Britannia.'

They had reached the sweep before the house and he had stopped the car and turned to look at her. 'And what have you to say to that?'

She gave him a long candid look. 'I'm wondering why you have brought me here to tea,' she said soberly.

He leaned across her and undid her safety belt, then kissed her hard. 'Perhaps I want to get to know you better,' he told her blandly as he got out.

She got out too, trying to look as though she wasn't wildly happy, excited and completely at sea, and walked beside him to the door. By the time they had mounted the half dozen shallow steps leading to it, it had been opened by a short stout man with a cheerful face, who answered the professor's greeting with a beaming smile, then turned the beam on

Britannia, and she, still in a delightful haze, beamed back.

The glass-walled lobby gave on to a square hall with a branched staircase at its far end and a number of doors on either side. It was a handsome apartment with a tiled floor spread with fine rugs and furnished with massive side tables bearing great bowls of flowers. Britannia looked about her with frank, un-selfconscious interest, wishing her father was with her to admire the fine ormolu clock on a marble-topped commode, the exquisite chandelier above her head, and the William and Mary armchairs set against the walls. She entered the room into which the professor was urging her with a lively anticipation of still more treasures, and she wasn't disappointed. It was large, lighted by great windows draped in claret-coloured velvet and with a polished floor adorned with still more silky rugs, but she had no time to examine her surroundings; there were two people there, sitting opposite each other beside the cheerful fire burning in the vast marble fire-place; a rather severe-looking lady who might have been in her sixties and the lovely girl who had been with the professor in church.

Britannia's pleasure ebbed away. Both ladies were eyeing her, the elder with a thoughtful expression, the younger with a smiling contempt, making her very aware of her slacks and anorak and sensible shoes, so that the pleasure was replaced by feminine rage at being caught at a disadvantage and an even greater rage towards the professor for allowing that to happen in the first place. She had time to wonder if he had done it deliberately before he said smoothly: 'Mama, this is Britannia Smith, without whose help I could not have saved the child I told you of. My mother, Britannia.'

Britannia shook hands and found that the severe features, relaxed in a smile, were rather charming after all; the blue eyes which looked at her so intently were very like the professor's and she found herself smiling back, conscious that she was approved of. It gave her a little added sparkle as she turned in obedience to the professor's suave: 'And this is Madeleine de Venz—you will have seen each other in church, I feel sure.'

They smiled brilliantly at each other; Madeleine's bright blue eyes were unfriendly as she looked Britannia slowly up and down. She said in a deliberate, sugary sweet voice: 'Of course, you were sitting with a pretty girl with curly hair.'

Britannia felt a surge of dislike. Several biting remarks crossed her mind and she longed to utter them. Her calm: 'Isn't she lovely? She's been a friend of mine for years,' was a masterpiece of forbearance. But the look she gave the professor was enough to freeze his bones, although he didn't appear to notice it.

His: 'We've come back for tea, Mama—I asked for it to be brought in here,' was uttered in exactly the right tones of a thoughtful host, as was his gentle urging that she should remove her anorak.

It was a pity that she happened to be wearing a blue guernsey, a garment which she had had for a number of years and wore solely for warmth during the winter at home. She had packed it at her mother's instigation and now silently blamed her parent for persuading her; it was a vast, loose sweater and seemed even bigger and looser than it was in contrast to Madeleine's slimly cut cashmere outfit, although, thought Britannia waspishly, the girl had a figure like a lead pencil, an opinion borne out when tea was brought in, for Madeleine drank only a small cup of milkless tea and ate nothing at all, while Britannia, telling herself sensibly that since she had been asked to tea she might as well enjoy it, ate the tiny sandwiches, the delicate cakes and the little sweet biscuits her host pressed upon her, carrying on a pleasant, desultory conversation with his mother while she did so, and when the professor chose to address her, answering him with cool politeness. Madeleine ignored her almost completely, addressing herself exclusively to the professor and speaking her own language until he interrupted her with a gentle: 'Should we not talk in English, Madeleine? You can hardly expect Britannia to understand Dutch after only a few days.'

Madeleine laughed, and she had a very pretty laugh,

'Darling Jake, I'm so sorry, you know I would do anything to please you.'

Britannia, watching him, couldn't see any change of expression in his face, but come to think of it, she seldom did. And she had learned one thing; he was called Jake, which was a name she entirely approved of. Quite pleased with this discovery, she plunged into a discussion about china. There was a handsome bowl on the table at her hostess's elbow—Weesp porcelain, she hazarded, and was pleased with herself when Mevrouw Luitingh van Thien, seeing her glance at it, began to talk of it; the subject led to a discussion about antiques in general until Britannia glanced at her watch and said, with real regret, that she would have to return to the Veskes' villa, and when the professor, sitting by Madeleine and engrossed in some conversation of his own, was apprised of this, she added matter-of-factly: 'It's no distance, and I shall enjoy the walk.'

'It's dark,' the professor pointed out flatly.

'There's a moon.' She added defiantly, 'And I like the dark.'

He took no notice of this, however, but got to his

feet, while Madeleine scowled at them all and then looked taken aback when Britannia went over to her. 'Forgive me, Juffrouw de Venz, for interrupting your talk with Professor Luitingh van Thien; it's only a few minutes' drive, though.' She added with sweet mendacity: 'I do hope that we meet again.'

But to her hostess she made no mention of hoping to see her again; she had been brought to the professor's home through some quirk of fancy on his part, she supposed, she wasn't likely to come again. She murmured all the right things and reflected wryly that at least she had had her wish; she had seen the house which had so taken her fancy and as an added bonus, she knew where the professor lived. She got into the anorak he was holding for her and accompanied him out to the car and got in without speaking when he opened the door. And she could think of nothing to say during the brief ride; it was all the more surprising, then, that when he stopped by the Veskes' front door and got out to open her door, instead of wishing him goodbye she should ask: 'Are you going to marry her?'

She wished she hadn't been so silly the moment the words were out; he would snub her coldly or not answer her at all.

He did neither. He said in a loud, forceful voice: 'No, I am not. Oh, at one time perhaps I considered it, but not any more—and do you know why, Miss

Britannia Smith? Because of you, and God alone knows why; you preach at me, disapprove of me, constantly remind me that I am selfish and bad-tempered, and now you have seen my home, you will probably mount a campaign to persuade me to give away every penny I have…and yet I find that without you my life and my heart are empty.'

Her heart bounced into her throat, almost choking her. 'Well, you know,' she said soberly, 'you may say all these things—and you have surprised me very much—but you don't behave as though you mean any of them. No man with any regard for a girl would take her to his home to meet his mother and the girl who intends to marry him without giving her the chance of at least doing her hair.' She added severely: 'I looked a perfect fright, and you know it.'

He said quite seriously: 'I thought you looked beautiful, Britannia. And I have just told you that I am not going to marry Madeleine.'

'Yes, I know, but she doesn't agree with that.' She shivered a little in the cold early dark. 'You see, she's right for you, Professor. She comes from your background and probably you have known each other for years, she will run your great house for you and entertain your guests and wear all the right clothes. She's beautiful, you know; all willowy and graceful…'

The professor caught her by the arm. 'Bah—who wants willows and grace? I like women to look like women, and pray, what is to prevent you entertaining our guests and running our home and wearing what you call the right clothes?'

His hand was still on her arm and she was very aware of it. She shook her head slowly and began deliberately to tear her dreams to shreds in a quiet, steady voice.

'I hoped that I would meet you again, even though I thought that you didn't like me, but I wanted to be sure of it, if you can understand that. You had told me that you were rich, remember? but I didn't bother about that, not until just now, sitting in your lovely home. But now I can see that just being rich isn't at all the same...' She came to a stop, anxious to find the right words. 'You see, you aren't just rich, Professor, it's more than that—it's a way of life; you live in a magnificent house which I think must have been in your family for a very long time; you drink your tea from Sèvres china and the chairs you sit on are a kind which any self-respecting museum would jump at. But you've been born and brought up among them, you've eaten from porcelain with silver knives and forks since you can remember, and that's the difference; you take them for granted, just as your Madeleine does, that's why she'll be right for you. Don't you see?'

'No.'

'Don't say no in that fashion, Professor!'

She heard him sigh. 'Britannia, before we go any further with this singlarly futile conversation, may I beg you to stop calling me Professor in that severe fashion. My name is Jake.'

'Yes, I know. I like it—but if I call you Jake, that's how I shall remember you…if I call you Professor you'll always be just that.'

'My dear girl, let us get one thing clear. I have no wish to be just a professor dwindling away in your thoughts. I'm a man called Jake who has fallen more than a little in love with you.'

'But if you hadn't met me, you would have married Madeleine.'

He took her gently by the shoulders. 'I'll give you an honest answer, Britannia, because I can't be anything else with you, you have been honest with me. Probably I should, but not because I loved her; I'm almost forty and I must have a wife and children to live in my home after me, but having said that, I'll repeat that now I have met you, I shall never marry her.'

'Never's a long time. I think this happens all the time—people meet and—and fall in love, perhaps not very deeply, and when circumstances prevent them meeting again, in time they forget and take up their lives as they were before.'

Britannia spoke with quiet conviction, not believing a word of it.

'You don't want to see me again?' the professor spoke harshly.

She stirred a little and his hands tightened their grip. 'Well, I shall never see you once I've gone back to England at the end of the week. Would it matter very much if we saw each other just once more, to say goodbye?'

'It's your own fault that we do say goodbye, you silly, stubborn, high-minded girl—and don't expect sympathy from me, for you'll get none.' He caught her close and kissed her so hard that she rocked on her feet and then without another word, marched her to the door, opened it and then turning away with a brief goodnight, got into his car and drove away.

Britannia went indoors, shutting the door silently behind her. There was a good deal of laughing and talking in the sitting room so that no one would have heard her come in. Half an hour in her room would give her a chance to pull herself together; it had been harder than she could have imagined because she loved the professor so much; too much, she reminded herself, to let him make a mistake he might regret later on. He had said that he was more than a little in love with her, but she wasn't sure if that was quite enough. Infatuation seemed like love, but it didn't last, and they had only met a few weeks ago and then only briefly. For herself she was quite sure that she loved him, but that wasn't enough either, although it was tempting to pretend that it was. She crossed the hall silently and was on the stairs when the sitting room door burst open and Joan ran out.

'I saw the car lights,' she cried. 'Britannia, never mind about going to your room; come into the sitting room and drink our health—Dirk and I are engaged, isn't it wonderful. He's got to go back in a few days, but he'll get leave and come back in six weeks' time and we'll get married then.' She caught Britannia by the arm and danced her into the sitting room, which seemed full of people all talking at once. Britannia went around shaking hands, laughing and talking with an animation she didn't feel, although two glasses of champagne did help. It was late by the time she got to bed; she had changed quickly and there had been a long-drawn-out dinner party with more champagne, so that her slightly muddled wits had been unable to cope with her own problems. But in the morning, after breakfast, it was easy enough to make an excuse about buying stamps while Joan wrote letters and telephoned her family. She put on the anorak once more and went along to get her bike. She had the morning before her, she would take one of the narrow country lanes where there was no traffic to bother her, and sort out her problems.

She was standing outside the front door, pulling up her anorak hood against the cold wind, when a Mini estate car drove up and stopped beside her, and the short stout man who had opened the door of the professor's home got out. His 'good morning' was cheerful as he handed her an envelope and stood waiting. Her name was scrawled on it and she knew it was from the professor, so that her fingers shook a little as she opened it. The note inside was brief: 'Will you come out to dinner with me this evening? Half past seven.' It was signed J. L. T.

'You will be so good as to give me the answer?' asked the patient man beside her.

'Will you please tell Professor Luitingh van Thien that I shall be delighted to accept.' It would be their last meeting, she guessed, and she had no intention of refusing.

'I was to tell you also, miss, that it is hoped that you will have sufficient time in which to make yourself ready.'

Britannia chuckled; the prospect of seeing the professor again had quite cheered her up, even though it hadn't solved any problems. Let those wait, she told herself defiantly. 'That's very considerate of the professor. Will you thank him for me? I don't know your name...?'

'Marinus, miss.' His cheerful beam swept over her. 'Good day, miss.'

'Good day, Marinus.' She watched him get into the Mini and drive away and then went back to the house to tell Mevrouw Veske that she would be out that evening; she had to face a barrage of questions, of course; her hostess, with her goddaughter's future nicely settled, wasn't averse to her friend doing the same thing.

Britannia cycled a long way, trying to make herself think sensibly. She was aware that she was being foolish in seeing the professor again; a strong-minded girl would have said goodbye then and there... She sighed and got off her machine, leaned it against a gate and went to sit on a fallen tree. It was dim and damp along the lanes; the trees, their leafless branches arched above her head, shutting out what winter light there was. But it exactly suited her mood. Her impulse to refuse to see the professor again once she had returned home had been right, she felt sure; the reasons were good sound ones and sensible, but that didn't make them any easier to accept for herself. As for him, very likely he would thank her in years to come.

Presently she got up again and began her ride back to the villa; there was lunch to be eaten, and the afternoon to get through before she could get ready for her evening. The pink dress, she reflected, although she very much doubted if the professor would notice it, but it would give her low morale a much-needed boost; the evening, she had determined, was going to be a success, something happy to remember for always. It was to be hoped that he wouldn't lose his temper or raise his voice; his note had been a little terse. She patted the pocket where she had put it and started to sing cheerfully, keeping her thoughts on the evening ahead and no further than that.

CHAPTER FIVE

BRITANNIA DRESSED with great care, with a meticulous attention to detail which would have done credit to an aristocrat on the way to the guillotine, and if truth were told, in very much the same mood. Fate and the kind fairies hadn't been so kind after all, or had they abandoned her because, with the professor in her hand, as it were, she had been too scrupulous?

She was ready far too soon and she went downstairs to sit with the Veskes, trying not to see Mevrouw Veske's coy glances while her host explained about the return trip he had booked for herself and Joan.

'Such a pity that you should have to return,' she observed, remorselessly interrupting her husband, 'but of course Joan will be with us again in a few weeks—perhaps you will be coming too, Britannia?' She added guilelessly: 'You also have friends here.'

Britannia gave her a limpid look. 'Oh, yes, you've all been so super—but Joan's only having a quiet wedding, no bridesmaids and only family and you, of course—besides, I've no more holidays due.'

Mevrouw Veske knitted a bit of complicated pattern with effortless ease. 'You might like to come back on your own account, my dear.'

'Oh, you mean work here?' said Britannia, carefully misunderstanding. 'Well, it might be fun, but there's always the language difficulty, and...' She paused thankfully as Berthe bounced in to say that the gentleman had arrived.

'Then show him in,' Mevrouw Veske begged her in her own language, and got up as she spoke to greet her visitor.

The professor was at his most charming and very elegant, his dark overcoat open to reveal a dinner jacket and shirt of pristine whiteness. Britannia, returning his cool greeting with one equally cool, thanked heaven that she had put on the pink dress; it was a little late in the day to capture his fancy— she seemed to have done that with nothing more glamorous than slacks and a sweater—but she felt well dressed and that made her feel confident. Ten minutes were spent in polite conversation before the professor got to his feet, murmuring that they had better make a start if they wanted their dinner, and Britannia went thankfully to fetch her coat. The professor helped her into it and just for a moment she wished that it had been mink or chinchilla instead of sensible tweed. Well, it wouldn't have made much difference, anyway, she told herself sensibly. But it seemed that her companion wasn't quite so unobservant as she had imagined. He shut the front door behind them, kissed her with quite surprising force and remarked: 'Don't complain—if you will dress up in that pink thing, you must expect the consequences. You're beautiful, Britannia.'

It was a promising start to the evening; she got into the car determined to make the most of what she had. Surely Madeleine wouldn't grudge her a few hours of happiness when she had a whole life-time before her, for despite the professor's protestations, Britannia thought the girl would somehow manage to marry him. She waited until he had got in beside her, then said: 'Thank you,' without either conceit or coyness.

'And thank God you don't simper,' observed her companion.

'And is that a compliment too?' she wanted to know severely.

He was taking the road south towards Arnhem. 'Ah, so my shortcomings are to be preached over, are they? My manners are at fault...'

'Don't be silly,' she begged him in a motherly voice. 'Your manners are very good indeed and you know that, and I'm not going to preach, truly I'm not.'

'Good. We're going to Scherpenzeel, just over twenty miles west of Arnhem. There's a delightful inn there. We can turn off the motorway just outside

Arnhem and go through Ede. I know it's dark, but at least there are villages. Do you find the motorways rather bleak?'

'Those I've been on, yes—I expect they vary.'

He said silkily: 'Shall we discuss them in depth—so safe a conversation, don't you agree?—or may we talk about ourselves?'

'Well, I don't much care to talk about roads,' said Britannia reasonably. 'But there's nothing to say about us—we've said it all.'

'You're being a silly girl again. Why do you suppose I've brought you out this evening?'

She kept her voice very steady. 'A sort of goodbye dinner, I thought.'

He gave a great laugh. 'I shan't say goodbye until the very last minute, Britannia, and that is still two days away. I shall spend the evening persuading you to marry me.'

The pink dress must be doing its work very well. She said in her calm way: 'That will be a waste of time, and you know it.'

'I shall have you in the end.'

She allowed a few seconds of delight at the prospect and then damped it down with common sense. 'Perhaps we had better talk about roads,' she observed primly.

They had swung off the motorway on to the road

to Ede, running through wooded country. 'We'll do no such thing. Tell me about your family.'

She began a little reluctantly, but he put skilful questions from time to time, so that she told him a good deal more than she had intended, although she stopped herself just in time from telling him just where her home was. She tried in her turn to ask questions too, without any success at all; his bland replies told her nothing; he had a mother, she knew that, but other than that she knew nothing about him and it was obvious that he had no intention of telling her; he kept the conversation strictly about herself and her own family until they arrived at Scherpenzeel.

De Witte Holevoet was an attractive inn, quite small but already almost full of people dining. The professor whisked Britannia inside, waited while she disposed of her coat before being shown to their table and then sat back in his chair to look at her. 'You're getting admiring glances from all the men in the room,' he assured her. 'It must be that pink thing—irresistible, isn't that the word?'

She answered him seriously, although her cheeks were as pink as her dress. 'That's what Mother always says.'

'And that is why you packed a pink dress to come to Holland?' His voice was bland, although she thought that he was amused.

She said defiantly: 'Yes.'

He smiled at her with a charm to melt her bones. 'I feel more hopeful. What would you like to drink?—we'll order presently.'

And from then on he kept the conversation light and impersonal, and she, cautious at first, presently realised that he wasn't going to talk about themselves at all—he had been joking about persuading her to marry him—she quenched quite unreasonable disappointment and followed his lead.

The meal was delicious; Britannia, who enjoyed her food, ate her way through lobster mousse, *Poulet au Champagne* and a lemon sorbet, helped along by a claret which even she, who knew very little about such things, realised was very fine. It was when they had finished their meal and she was pouring their coffee that she asked suddenly: 'Have you a dog?'

'Two—you didn't see them at my home because they were in the kitchen having their meal. Why do you ask?'

She handed him his coffee. 'Well, I just wanted to know something about you...'

'You will have every opportunity of knowing everything about me when we are married.' He was smiling at her and she didn't suppose that he was serious.

'What sort of dogs?' she persisted; anxious to seem as lighthearted as he, she smiled back at him.

'A Bouvier and a Corgi. They're the best of friends.' He added, still smiling: 'My housekeeper has a cat, and the gardener's children have rabbits and a tortoise.'

'Where does the gardener live? I saw a dear little house up against the wall when I cycled there...'

He nodded. 'That is his home. Marinus and Emmie—the housekeeper—and his wife, live in the house, so do a couple of maids. The laundrywoman lives in the other cottage.'

Her eyes were round. 'The laundrywoman—that sounds quite feudal! She surely doesn't do all the laundry for that great place.'

'Lord, no—just the personal things. I don't allow anyone else to iron my shirts.'

'Why, you are feudal!'

His smile mocked her. 'Disapproving? There are a great many things you don't approve of, aren't there, Britannia? But none of them matter, you know, and if you think about it, it's fair enough—old Celine does my shirts, and when she's ill, I look after her.'

She had to admit that that was true enough and he added in a wheedling tone: 'I'm quite a nice chap, really.'

'That isn't what you said in London. You told me that you were rich and something of a hermit and you didn't need to please anyone.'

'Ah, I wanted you to know the worst first.'

She laughed at that, but he didn't say any more, but began to tell her about the nearby castle of Scherpenzeel. 'It's owned by a family with the impressive name of van der Bosch-Royaards van Scherpenzeel, but no one lives there. It's neo-Gothic and I think rather nice.'

'Not as nice as your house. What is it called?'

'Huize van Thien.'

She asked meekly: 'May I know something about it?'

He passed his cup for more coffee. 'The oldest part is thirteenth-century, the whole of the front was added in the eighteenth century. The round tower at the back is fifteenth-century, its rooms are furnished, but we only use the sitting room on the ground floor.'

'Who's we?'

'You remind me of a schoolteacher examining her class! Myself, my mother when she is staying with me and my three sisters when they pay me a visit.'

'Three sisters?' repeated Britannia, much struck with this homely piece of information. 'You're the eldest, of course.'

'Yes.' He went on blandly, 'I prefer the newest part of the house; they built roomily in the eighteenth century and their enormous windows let in the light. Tell me about your home, Britannia.'

She really had no choice after all her questions, and anyway, there would be thousands of small houses like her own home, there would be no fear of him discovering where it was. 'It's very small, a late Georgian cottage, built of stone with a slate roof. There's quite a big garden, though, with some rather ramshackle outbuildings. There are woods all round us and it's very peaceful, even in summer; the tourists don't come near us, only if they lose their way, and the village is so small there isn't even an hotel, just a pub.'

'I like your English pubs,' said the professor idly. 'What's this one called?'

'The Happy Return.' She hadn't meant to tell him that, she would have to guard her tongue, though it was a common enough name, and besides, why was she worrying? Once she had gone, he wouldn't come after her; he would see, as soon as they had parted, that the whole episode was just a pleasant little interlude. She had thought it so often that she almost believed it herself.

They lingered over their coffee and returned by a different road, across the Veluwe and a good deal further round, but as the professor pointed out, it was a charming route once they were through Barneveld, taking them through the National Park along a minor road which, he assured her, was quite delightful in daylight. So they didn't arrive back at the

Veskes' villa until well after midnight, to find the house in darkness excepting for a welcoming light shining from the hall window. The professor got out and walked round the car to open her door. 'You have a key?'

'Yes.' She gave it to him and as he put it in the lock, said: 'Thank you for a lovely evening. I did enjoy it.'

He didn't open the door. 'We shall have many lovely evenings and enjoy them too, Britannia.'

She didn't know how beautiful she looked under the dim light streaming from the hall. She stared up at him and said earnestly: 'Please, Jake—I'm only a passing fancy.'

His face darkened. 'So I'm to be preached at again, am I? I don't know why I stand for it; how can you know what I want and what I think, and who are you to tell me what I must do and not do? I'll tell you: you're a sharp-tongued obstinate woman who thinks she knows best and spends her time poking her nose into my affairs so that I lose my temper.'

He opened the door and held it wide. 'In with you.' His voice was a muttered roar as she went past him and heard the door shut behind her. She had gone perhaps six paces when the door-knocker was thumped and she flew back to open the door before the whole house was roused.

'Such a noise!' she told him severely. 'You'll wake everyone, it's long past...'

'Not another word,' he said softly. 'I forgot something.'

He caught her close and kissed her slowly. Presently he loosened his hold a little. 'Will you come out to dinner with me tomorrow, Britannia?' And when she hesitated: 'You go home the day after. I'll behave exactly as I ought and we will say goodbye very correctly.' His voice was gentle, but she had the strange idea that he was laughing too, although when she looked up into his face it was serious enough. She found it quite impossible to say no, and indeed, she had no wish to say it. She nodded her head without speaking and he kissed her again, this time very gently, and pushed her just as gently into the hall and shut the door. She heard the car slide away a few seconds later.

Mevrouw Veske received the news that Britannia was going out again with the professor with delighted satisfaction. She didn't exactly say 'I told you so,' but Britannia could see her thinking it and the speculative look in her hostess's eye made her wonder if she was already envisaging a double wedding. She spent the day with her in Apeldoorn, shopping, arriving back at the same time as an excited Joan, who had spent the day with Dirk. She was flourishing her new engagement ring and teatime talk was almost exclusively of its unique beauty, the forthcoming wedding and the future bride's speculations as to what exactly she should wear for the occasion, so that when it was time for Britannia to go to her room and change for the evening, she was able to do so with only the smallest amount of interest from her companions.

The professor was in the hall, having just been admitted by Berthe, when she came downstairs, and as she went towards him she said with disarming frankness: 'I've only one dress with me, I hope you don't mind—you see, I didn't expect...' She paused, remembering why she had brought it with her in the first place, so that he looked enquiringly at her.

'Then why did you bring it?' he wanted to know. It didn't occur to her not to tell him the truth.

'It's a silly reason.' She was standing in front of him, looking up into his face. 'I thought—that is, I imagined that if I did meet you again, I'd like to be wearing something pretty, so that you would— would notice me.' She added seriously: 'Of course, I didn't know then about your house and your Madeleine...'

'Not my Madeleine. I think that I should have noticed you if you had been wearing an old sack, Britannia.'

She smiled a little shyly. 'Oh—well...I didn't know that, did I?'

'No. Are we really saying goodbye tomorrow, Britannia?'

'Yes.' She moved away and began to fasten her coat, and felt hurt when he said quite cheerfully:

'In that case, we'd better start our evening, hadn't we?'

They were seen off by a beaming Mevrouw Veske and a hasty wave and gabbled ''bye' from Joan, who was, as she so often was these days, on the telephone to her Dirk, and once in the car the professor observed dryly: 'What a pity it is that you don't share Mevrouw Veske's romantic outlook—now, if you did you might have come tearing down the stairs and flung yourself into my arms, instead of which you greet me with some matter-of-fact remark about your dress. What's wrong with it, anyway?'

Britannia was put out. 'There's nothing wrong with it—it's a copy of a model, a Jean Allen—but one doesn't usually wear the same dress on two successive evenings.'

He had turned the car in the direction of Apeldoorn. 'Why ever not? I wear my dinner jacket for several evenings in a row.'

She chuckled. 'Now you're being silly.' She didn't add that there was nothing she would have liked better than to have flung herself into his arms. 'But I was glad to see you.' And then, in case he had an answer to that, she asked quickly: 'Have you had a busy day?'

'Quite a list...' He began to tell her about the cases and it wasn't until they were through Hoenderloo that he paused to say: 'We're not going to Apeldoorn, by the way. There's a restaurant on the Amersfoort road that's quite good. I thought we had better not go too far this evening, I expect you have your packing to do.'

A damping remark which lowered her spirits considerably; she could pack, if necessary, in ten minutes and she would have all tomorrow in which to do it...

She thought his description of De Echoput was sadly understated when they reached it; it was a rather splendid place and the menu card quite baffling in its abundance. Over their drinks she studied it and presently asked the professor to choose for her. 'Because there's so much and I don't know the half of the dishes they offer,' she explained. 'You see now what I mean about our backgrounds—imagine having a wife who doesn't know what *Le Râble de Lièvre* is—it's hare, I know, but I don't know more than that.' She added thoughtfully: 'I don't like hare, anyway; I like to see them running in the fields.'

He smiled at her across the table. 'So do I, and

would it really matter if you can't read the menu if I'm with you to help you choose?'

She shook her head. 'It wouldn't be as simple as that, and you know it.'

He didn't answer her, only smiled again and turned to the menu. 'They have delicious hors d'oeuvres here, shall we start with that—and what about trout? *Truite saumone au Champagne*. We'll drink champagne, too, since it's by way of being an occasion.'

The food was delicious, just as he had said, but Britannia hardly enjoyed it—he had called it an occasion, almost as though he was celebrating... It cost her quite an effort to join in his cheerful talk. Luckily the champagne helped, so that by the time the sweet trolley came round she was able to do full justice to the millefeuille recommended by the professor and, just for a little while, forget that she would never see him again.

Sitting over their coffee he brought the conversation round to her return.

'You'll be working next week?' he wanted to know, 'or do you go home for a few days?'

The champagne had made Britannia a little careless. 'I start work on Monday,' she told him. 'Even if I didn't, it would be too far to go home. I'll wait until I get my weekend.'

'You plan to stay at St Jude's?'

She stirred her coffee and didn't look at him. 'I haven't thought about it. Probably not.'

His voice was bland. 'Of course, the world is your oyster, isn't it, Britannia? A qualified nurse can go where she pleases.'

Put like that it sounded a lonely business; going from hospital to hospital, probably country to country, getting a little older with each move. She swallowed a great wave of self-pity and heard him say briskly: 'Well, you don't need to look so glum; think how fortunate you are compared with a girl who marries; a house to run, a husband to look after, children to bring up, never-ending chores—the poor girl has no life of her own.'

She didn't want a life of her own, but it wasn't much use saying so; hadn't she made it quite clear that she had no intention of marrying him? She asked in a rather high voice: 'Did you never want to travel?'

He seemed quite willing to follow her lead; they carried on a desultory conversation about nothing in particular until Britannia said that she thought she should return to the Veskes. 'They're so kind,' she spoke brightly. 'We've done exactly what we've wanted to do all the time we've been staying with them, it's been a wonderful holiday.'

He had opened the car door for her and paused to ask: 'And one to remember, Britannia?'

She would never forget it, however hard she tried. She babbled: 'Oh, rather, it's been lovely.' She went on babbling for the entire journey back and the professor tiresomely did nothing to stop her; by the time they had reached the villa she was worn out and so exasperated that she could have burst into tears, although why she wasn't quite sure. He had behaved exactly as he should have done; he hadn't mentioned seeing her again; he had accepted the fact that she was going back to England with no apparent disappointment. Either he was a man of iron with no feelings, or he hadn't meant a word...

Britannia slept badly and got up the next morning with a frayed temper and a pale face, and it didn't help when she found herself drawn into a cheerful discussion about Joan's wedding; indeed, a good deal of the morning was spent in reviewing the arrangements already made, re-making them, adding to them and speculating as to the weather, the number of guests and the names of those who just had to be invited, and when this serious business had been thoroughly talked out, there was always the more interesting one of clothes for the important occasion. By the time lunch was over Britannia, her nerves jangling like an ill-tuned piano and longing to be by herself, declared that she simply couldn't leave Holland without one more cycle ride, and since they weren't leaving until the evening and she was packed and ready, except for exchanging her slacks and sweater for her suit, she had ample time to indulge her fancy, and Joan and Mevrouw Veske, deep in the merits of various pastel shades, begged her kindly to do just as she wished. 'Only don't be late for tea,' counselled Joan. 'We shall be leaving round about six o'clock, love.'

Britannia promised, tugged on her hostess's anorak and gloves and went round to fetch her bike. The day had been overcast, but now it was clearing, to show a cold blue sky turning grey at the edges, and the wind, never absent for long, had gathered strength again. It surprised her to find that it was icy underfoot, but going cautiously down the drive she decided that she was safe enough. The lanes she intended to take were sheltered by the trees and thickets and their surfaces rough, and she was a seasoned cyclist. She knew where she was going, of course—to take one more look at the professor's home. She wouldn't be able to see much of it, only its gables and chimney pots, but they were better than nothing.

It would have helped, she reflected as she pedalled down the deserted road, if he had wished her goodbye. But he hadn't. He had got out of his car and gone to the Veskes' door with her and opened it, listened to her over-bright thanks with a little smile, assured her that he had enjoyed his evening just as much as she had, wished her the most casual of goodnights without once expressing a wish to see her again, and then stood aside so that she might go in. She couldn't remember what she had mumbled, certainly nothing of sufficient interest to make him delay his departure. She had gone past him into the hall, afraid that she might burst into tears at any moment, and had heard the door close quietly behind her. There was no knock this time, either; she had heard the soft purr of the Rolls almost immediately, and its almost soundless departure.

She reached the crossroads and turned down the lane. There was still masses of time; she would be able to go further along the wall where the view of the house was much clearer. The lane was a bit tricky, its surface slippery between the ruts, but she went slowly, putting out a leg from time to time to steady herself. She paused as she reached the first vantage point. There was smoke rising from some of the chimneys, blown wildly by the wind, and she wondered who was there. Not Jake, he had mentioned that he had a teaching round in the afternoon and some private patients to see, but his mother perhaps and possibly the beautiful Madeleine, invited there to spend the evening. She might even be staying there. Britannia shivered; the wind was really icy and a few drops of sleet from a sky which had suddenly turned grey again made her wonder if she wouldn't be wise to turn back. But the gap in the wall wasn't far, it was a pity to come that distance and give up within half a mile. She mounted her machine once more and pedalled on.

It was worth it, she told herself, when she stopped once more. The house, light shining from its windows in the gathering dusk, looked beautiful. She imagined the cheerful Marinus trotting to and fro about his stately business and Jake's mother sitting by the fire—she would be embroidering, something complicated and beautiful, to be handed down to other generations of the family in course of time. Britannia, deep in thought, mounted her bike once more, turned too sharply, skidded on an icy patch and fell off. She fell awkwardly and the machine fell on top of her, the handlebars catching her on the side of the head as she hit the ground, and knocking her out.

She came to quite quickly, feeling muzzy, and lay still for a minute, waiting for her head to clear before she attempted to get up. She was aware that she had a nasty headache, rapidly turning into an unpleasant throbbing, and she was also aware of the bitter cold.

'Well, it won't do to lie here, my girl,' she admonished herself in a heartening voice. 'Get to your feet, warm yourself up and get on your bike and go back as fast as you can.'

Sound advice, but not, she discovered, so easy to

carry out. The cycle had fallen across her and she had to wriggle to one side to get free of it, and it was when she began to do this that she discovered that her left ankle was exquisitely painful. She essayed to move it cautiously, and a wave of nausea swept over her so that she was forced to keep still again.

'Clever girl,' said Britannia crossly, 'broken your ankle, have you, or sprained it? Well, you'll just have to roll yourself to one side.'

It took a few minutes, because the pain was bad and her headache was worsening, but she managed it at last and presently she essayed to sit up, but she jarred the ankle badly doing it and this time the pain made her do something she had never in her life done before—faint.

She came to presently and found herself wishing that she could have remained unconscious for a little longer, for her headache was steadily worsening and the pain in her ankle was making her feel sick. Nevertheless she tried to think what to do; she wouldn't be missed for a little while yet, and even when she was, no one would have the least idea where to start looking for her. Somehow or other she would have to get herself back to the road. She wasn't sure how she was going to do it, because it was at least a mile and the lane would be heavy going. She could try shouting, she supposed, and remembered that the professor had told her that there were no houses nearby. The gardener's cottage she had seen was, she judged, too far off for anyone there to hear her, but it was worth a try. She called 'Help!' several times, upsetting the birds in the thicket around her and listening to her voice being carried away on the wind before deciding that it was a waste of time and breath. She would have to get moving and hope for the best.

She turned herself a little and looked at her ankle. It was already swollen; to get her shoe off would lessen the pain, on the other hand, she would need it for protection against the lane's deplorable surface, and not only that, it was getting colder every minute and darker too. She rolled over once more and edged herself forward. She had no idea how long she had been crawling along so painfully when her injured ankle brushed against a sharp stone and she fainted again.

Tea was almost finished in the Veskes' household before Joan remarked: 'Britannia's awfully late—I wonder if she's in her room? I'll see.'

She came downstairs again looking faintly worried. 'She's not there. I wonder where she went? Not to Hoenderloo, I remember she said she wouldn't be going that way because I asked her to post a letter...' She looked at her godmother. 'Where does she go when she goes off on the bike?'

Mevrouw Veske thought deeply. 'Well, dear, she has made a number of acquaintances, but not the sort who would go for a cycle ride with her. I daresay she goes on her own.' Her nice face cleared. 'How stupid of me—I expect she's gone to say goodbye to that nice Professor Luitingh van Thien. He's taken her out two evenings running, you know, and they seem to be getting on very well together,' and when Joan was about to interrupt her: 'Yes, dear, you're surprised, but I'm sure she's had very little time to tell you about that. You've been out a good deal yourself and there's been the wedding to talk of. Shall I telephone him? He'll be in the book and we have met, although we're hardly on calling terms, I suppose.'

'I'll go,' said Joan, and as she left the room: 'Will he be home?'

'I've no idea, but I believe it's a very large house, there's bound to be someone in it.' Mevrouw Veske got to her feet. 'I'll do it, Joan. If they don't understand English it will be a little difficult for you.'

A man answered her call, introduced himself as the house butler and told her that Miss Smith hadn't been to the house that afternoon. 'Although I will inform the professor when he returns; he may know something, *mevrouw*. If I might call you back?'

* * *

Marinus replaced the receiver, his cheerful face frowning in thought. The professor had returned home on the previous night in a towering rage all the more formidable for being held in check. He had gone straight to his room and that morning had left early for his consulting rooms in Arnhem, leaving no messages at all and certainly none about Miss Smith. Marinus trod with rather more speed than usual across the hall and down the passage which led to the kitchens, where he found Emmie busy at the kitchen table. He unburdened himself at some length and then asked her advice.

Emmie didn't pause in her folding of a soufflé mixture. 'Telephone him at once,' she suggested. 'He will wish to know, I think, for he is very interested in this English lady, is he not?'

Marinus looked at his old-fashioned pocket watch. 'He will be at his rooms, he will have patients…'

His wife began to pour her mixture into a buttered and papered dish. 'Telephone him,' she repeated.

Marinus had to wait a moment or two before he could speak to the professor; there was a patient with him, explained his secretary, who would be gone in a very short time; just time enough to give Marinus the leisure to wonder if he was being needlessly foolish. After all, Miss Smith was returning to England that very evening and the professor hadn't even mentioned the fact; perhaps dear Emmie was wrong.

But she wasn't, he could tell that by the sound of the professor's voice when he started asking questions. How long had Miss Smith been gone? Had Mevrouw Veske said anything about searching for her? Had she been warmly clad?

Marinus, being unable to answer any of these enquiries with any degree of accuracy, was told sharply to see that the professor's horse was saddled and ready for him, together with a torch and blanket. 'I shall be home almost immediately, and I want the dogs as well.'

'You know where Miss Smith is?' asked Marinus.

'I believe so.' The professor's voice sounded harsh as he replaced the receiver.

He was as good as his word. Caesar, his great roan horse, was being led round to the front door as he got out of the Rolls and went indoors. Marinus, hovering in the hall, hurried to meet him. 'I've put out your riding things, Professor—' he began, to be cut short with: 'No time. I'll go as I am. Telephone Mevrouw Veske, will you, and see that there's a room ready just in case Miss Smith needs to stay the night.'

He had gone again, taking Caesar at a careful trot down the drive, the dogs at his heels.

It was a dark evening and the overhanging trees

made it even darker. The professor kept the beam from his torch steady, not bothering to turn its light from side to side of the road, he was so sure where Britannia would be. He urged his horse along now, holding the reins with easy assurance, his face without expression, giving no hint of the mounting impatience he felt. At the crossroads he was forced to slow down, for the ground had become even more treacherous, but he whistled to the dogs and urged them on ahead, watching their progress. He paused for a moment where he and Britannia had first stopped, but there was no sign of her and he went on again, searching the thicket on either side of him until he heard Jason's deep bark and Willy's excited yap. He could just make them out by the torch's light, standing one each side of Britannia, sprawled across the lane.

The professor swung himself off his horse with the agility of a much younger man and knelt down beside her. Britannia was still unconscious. Her white face, with a nasty bruise down one side of it, looked quite alarming by the light of the torch, but the professor wasted no time in exclaiming over her appearance. He took her pulse, found it to be strong and regular, noted her grossly swollen ankle and said briskly: 'Wake up, Britannia, we have to get you home.'

He repeated himself several times, interlarded

with several pungent remarks in his own language although Britannia, recalled to consciousness by the insistence of his voice, really had no idea of what he was saying. She opened her eyes to find him staring down at her, looking so formidable that she frowned and closed her eyes again. She opened them almost immediately though, because there were two dogs looking at her too. She said in a very small voice: 'The Bouvier and the Corgi,' and then: 'You're wearing a good suit…it'll be spoilt.'

The professor didn't smile. He said something forceful in his own language again and Britannia thought it prudent not to ask what it was. She said helpfully: 'I've hurt my ankle. I'm sorry I can't walk, I crawled for a while, but I don't think I got very far. If you wouldn't mind just helping me to the end of the lane, I'd be all right there while you go and telephone Mijnheer Veske. He'll take me to hospital and they can strap it…'

The professor was busy; he had cut the shoe lace of the sensible shoe she was wearing and was carefully slicing it open so that he could ease it off her injured ankle. He held her foot steady in one large gentle hand and worked with the other, and only when she stopped talking because the pain was so bad did he speak. 'Stop issuing instructions like a demented great-aunt, Britannia. You must know that I shan't listen to a word of them, nonsensical as they are. And now grit your teeth, my girl, this is going to hurt.'

It did, but she didn't utter a sound, only shivered and shook and felt sick, and then, when the shoe was off and she felt the warmth of the blanket about her, so relieved that the tears she had so sternly held in check escaped at last.

Her rescuer turned the torch on her face then and examined the bruise, muttering to himself so that she managed at last: 'Please don't be so angry, Jake, I know it's awkward—I mean meeting again after we've said goodbye.' Some of her spirit returned. 'And it's very rude to mutter and mumble so that no one knows what you're saying.'

'You want to know what I was saying?' He picked her up effortlessly, although she was a big girl. 'That if you had listened carefully, you would know that I didn't say goodbye.'

He strode over to where Caesar stood waiting and Britannia let out a squeak of surprise. 'A horse— he's huge!' She added apprehensively: 'I can't get up there...'

He didn't even bother to answer; she was lifted and laid across the great beast's neck and while she was still panicking about holding on, the professor had swung himself up behind her, picked up the reins, whistled to the dogs and had turned for home.

He went slowly and carefully, but all the same

her ankle was agonisingly painful. It was quite dark now and the road when they reached it was deserted. She said suddenly: 'It's a good thing it's dark, we must look quite extraordinary.' She gave a tired little chuckle and when he didn't speak, she asked: 'Are you still angry?'

His voice came from the darkness above her. 'I am not angry.'

She drew a sharp breath as Caesar stumbled on a stone and she felt the professor's arm, holding her firmly round the shoulders, tighten. After a moment he said quietly: 'We're almost home.'

He hadn't once spoken a word of sympathy, she reflected in a rather woolly fashion. Any other man...but then any other man might have wasted time doing just that, while he had done everything possible with a swift efficiency and a minimum of talk, and he had known where to find her... She was framing a question about that when Caesar came to a halt and she was aware of lights and voices.

Being lifted down was a painful business; Britannia gritted her teeth and kept her eyes shut as the professor carried her indoors, suddenly too tired to mind about anything anymore.

CHAPTER SIX

HALFWAY UP the staircase Britannia roused herself sufficiently to say: 'I'm too heavy,' but the professor didn't speak, keeping up a steady, unhurried pace until he reached the gallery above. Emmie was ahead of him, ready with the door open of a room at its end. She had the bed turned down too and a blanket spread on it on to which he laid Britannia, who, feeling its warm security and seeing Emmie's kind face peering at her, not surprisingly went immediately to sleep.

She didn't sleep for long, although when she woke it was to find that someone had got her out of her clothes and put her in a nightgown; she vaguely remembered lifting arms and raising her head and Emmie's voice murmuring comfortingly, and now she lay, nicely propped up with pillows, the bedcovers turned back, disclosing an ugly, swollen ankle. She was frowning at it when Emmie came back with the professor at her heels.

His 'Hullo, feeling better?' was laconic, but his examination of her foot was meticulous and very gentle. He hadn't quite finished when Britannia asked: 'Please will you telephone Mijnheer Veske?

125

If someone could lend me a dressing gown he could take me to Arnhem...'

'And what do you propose to do in Arnhem?' the professor wanted to know without bothering to look at her.

'Well, get this strapped, then...'

'I believe that I am still capable of strapping an ankle.' His voice was silky.

'Oh, I'm sure you are,' soothed Britannia. 'What I mean is, I wanted to get away from here—at least, I don't want to, if you see what I mean, but it would be so much nicer for you.'

'You have a quite nasty contusion over your left eye, probably a little concussion as a consequence, which would account for your muddled conversation.'

Indeed her head did ache; she had done her best and she suspected that her ankle would become even more painful before it was strapped. 'I don't feel quite the thing,' she admitted.

'That is hardly surprising.' He sounded austere. 'I am going to strap that ankle. It is a sprain. I was able to take a look at it while you were in a faint. Tomorrow you will go to the hospital and have an X-ray of it, and also of your head.'

'But I'm going home—all the arrangements...' Her tired head whirled at the very thought.

'Leave the arrangements to me. You'll not be go-

ing home for a few days. And now let us attend to
your ankle.'

Britannia lay still, willing herself not to let out so
much as a squeak of pain. She clasped Emmie's kind
hand and squeezed it hard, and when the professor
had finally done, thanked him in a trembly voice.

She got a grunt in reply and an injunction to drink
the tea which would be fetched to her and then to
go to sleep. 'There's nothing much wrong with your
head that a good sleep won't cure,' remarked the
professor with impersonal kindness.

She opened her eyes to look at him, leaning over
the end of the bed, staring at her. 'Then I don't need
to have it X-rayed tomorrow—I've put you to
enough trouble.'

'And probably will put me to a great deal more.'
He nodded carelessly and went to the door, and Emmie drew up a chair and sat down by the bed. It
didn't matter that she couldn't speak a word of English; she helped Britannia to drink her tea, shook
up her pillows for her and then held her in a comfortable embrace while she cried her eyes out. She
felt better after that and went to sleep almost at once,
her head, very tousled, still against Emmie's plump
shoulder.

She woke hours later to a darkened room lighted
by a bedside lamp, by which the professor was reading. He looked up almost immediately and came to

the bed, took her pulse, looked at her pupil reactions, turned her head gently to examine the great bruise colouring one side of it and asked: 'How do you feel, Britannia?'

She studied his face before she replied. His calm expression gave no hint as to his feelings. She sighed: 'Not at all bad, thank you. My head feels much better—my ankle's a bit painful but quite bearable. What's the time?'

'Two o'clock. Emmie has some soup for you, you will drink it and go to sleep again.'

'Two...but you ought to be in bed, you'll be tired out in the morning.'

There was the glimmer of a smile on his face. 'I shall go to bed very shortly. Here is Emmie.'

The housekeeper looked even cosier than she did by day, wrapped in a thick woollen dressing gown. She bore a small tray upon which was a pipkin of soup, a dazzling white napkin and a glass of lemonade. The soup smelled delicious and Britannia's pinched nose wrinkled in anticipation. The professor stood, book in hand, one long finger marking his place, while Emmie arranged Britannia's pillows, tucked the napkin under her chin, removed the pipkin's lid and offered her the soup. Only when Britannia had taken the first spoonful did he go to the door and with a quiet 'Goodnight, Britannia,' go out of the room. Undoubtedly he was annoyed at her

having to be in his house at all. He was a good host
and a good surgeon so she would receive nothing
but courtesy and the best of attention while she was
there, but that was all. Her lip quivered and tears
filled her lovely eyes and she put the spoon down,
to be at once comforted by Emmie's *'Nou, nou,'* and
the offer of a clean handkerchief. 'Drink,' commanded Emmie with kindly firmness and Britannia
picked up her spoon once more. She drank down the
lemonade too because her attendant expected her to,
but by then she was feeling tired again and her head
was aching. She had barely thanked Emmie before
she was asleep again.

It was daylight when she awoke for the second
time, the curtains drawn to show a bright morning,
a fire crackling in the steel grate. Britannia sat up
cautiously and looked around her. She felt much better. There would be no need for her to be X-rayed
and she would say so; she would also have to find
out what had happened to Joan and whether she was
to get back to the Veskes that morning...and when
would she be able to go back to England? She
closed her eyes and frowned, then opened them
again to have a good look at the room she was in.

It was a large, airy room, with two tall windows
draped in rose pink silk, a colour echoed in the bed-
cover of quilted chintz and the upholstered armchairs, the furniture was painted white picked out

with gilt and the floor was carpeted in a soft misty blue, very restful to the eye. A charming room, and luxurious. Britannia closed her eyes once more and wondered what could be the time. She opened them almost at once, though, because someone was knocking at the door, and in answer to her 'Come in', Mevrouw Luitingh van Thien entered.

'Good morning, my dear,' she said, and smiled. 'Jake told me to wait until you were awake before giving you your breakfast. I'm glad to see that you have slept. Emmie is coming in a few minutes with tea and toast for you—he said to give you nothing more than that until you have been to hospital. He will be back for you at ten o'clock.'

'Oh—I was going to ask him if I need be X-rayed. I feel so much better.'

The professor's parent shook her elegant head. 'Oh, I shouldn't do that if I were you.' She sat herself down in a chair close by the bed. 'One must always do as one's doctor says.'

Britannia was on the point of saying that the professor wasn't her doctor anyway, but stopped herself in time because it might have sounded rude. Instead she thanked her companion for her kindness in offering her shelter for the night.

Mevrouw Luitingh van Thien looked surprised and then laughed. 'But, my dear child, it had nothing to do with me, this is Jake's house. I stay with him from time to time, that is all. When he left this morning he put you into my care and I am more than happy to do what I can for you. I have three daughters of my own, you know, they are all married and I can assure you that when they are all here with their husbands and children, it is indeed a houseful, something Jake enjoys very much.'

'Does he?' cried Britannia in surprise. 'I thought—that is, he never seems...'

Mevrouw Luitingh van Thien's features relaxed into a smile again. 'No, he doesn't does he?' she agreed. 'And yet he loves children and his home and family.'

'He told me that he was something of a hermit,' said Britannia indignantly.

'Well, so he is, if by that he means that he doesn't have a busy social life or escort a variety of young women to some night club or other far too often.' The lady's tone made it plain what she thought of night clubs. 'He enjoys a pleasant life; he has a great many friends and he loves his work, as you have no doubt seen for yourself.' She broke off to say: 'Ah, here is Emmie, I will leave you to enjoy your breakfast. When you have finished, she will help you to dress.'

It was only when she was at the door that Britannia remembered to ask: 'I quite forgot to ask you.

What did Mevrouw Veske say? And has Joan, my friend, you know—gone back?'

'Of course—I forgot too—I was to tell you that Mevrouw Veske will be over to see you this afternoon, and Joan has returned as it had been arranged. She will see the *Directrice* of your hospital and explain what happened. You may be sure that Jake has not overlooked anything.'

Britannia tackled her breakfast with a healthy appetite, her painful ankle notwithstanding, and when Emmie came back presently with her clothes, brushed and neat, she began the business of getting them on cheerfully enough. The problem of washing had been solved by Emmie bringing a basin to the bedside, but dressing didn't prove quite as easy as she had expected. But somehow she wriggled and twisted her way into her slacks and sweater, pausing for minutes at a time to allow the pain in her ankle to lessen, and the slacks had had to be cut in order to get her swollen foot into the leg. More or less dressed, she surveyed her person carefully and deplored her appearance. Emmie had brushed her hair and tied it back and then fetched a mirror reluctantly enough, and when Britannia saw her face in it she quite understood why; she was a sorry sight, one side of her face swollen and discoloured and a bump on her forehead the size of a billiard ball. Even if the professor had taken a fancy to her, which he hadn't, it would have needed to have been a very strong fancy. She was still staring at her reflection when he said from the doorway: 'May I come in?' and then: 'You're going to have a black eye.'

He said something to Emmie, asked: 'Are you ready?' and scooped Britannia up and carried her downstairs to the car. He had very much the manner, she considered, of a man removing a misbehaving kitten to the garden; kind, firm and faintly resigned that he had had to do it in the first place.

He stowed her into the front seat beside him while Emmie and Marinus proffered cushions with which to protect her foot. This done to his satisfaction, he got in, asked her in a rather perfunctory manner if she were quite comfortable and drove to Arnhem, wasting no breath in conversation on the way and wasting no time either. Britannia, seeking in vain for a topic of conversation and unable to think of anything at all to say, was relieved when they reached the hospital, where he lifted her from the car and set her in the wheelchair a porter was sent to fetch. She felt at a distinct disadvantage with no make-up, her hair austerely brushed back by Emmie and Mevrouw Veske's amply cut anorak dragged on anyhow; moreover, there was no vestige of glamour about a wheelchair. Not that it mattered; the professor muttered to the porter, said 'I'll see you in a minute,' and stalked away, leaving her to be trundled to X-ray, past a long line of fractured arms and legs, broken collarbones, barium meals and the like, all waiting patiently for their turn. Presumably this wasn't to be her lot; she was taken directly into the X-ray room where she was arranged on the table by a pretty nurse who nodded and smiled at her and then melted into the background as a thick-set bearded man and the professor ranged themselves beside her.

'That is indeed a splendid bruise,' observed the bearded man cheerfully. 'Let us hope that there is no hairline fracture beneath it.' He smiled broadly and held out a hand. 'Berens—Frans Berens.' He wrung her hand in a crushing grip and turned to the professor. 'The skull first, I think, Jake, and then the ankle.'

It was quickly done, but she was told to stay where she was while the plates were developed, and lay, cosily wrapped in a blanket in the half dark, half asleep until the professor's voice caused her to open her eyes.

'No bones broken,' he told her, 'just a nasty sprain. Bed for a few days and then massage and exercises.'

'But can't I go home?'

Doctor Berens rumbled disapprovingly. 'Indeed you cannot. You have had a nasty fall and you must have time to get over it; besides, that ankle must lose its swelling...'

'You will return with me, Britannia,' stated the professor in a no-nonsense voice, 'and when you are fit, you may return home.'

'To the Veskes?'

'I imagine not—they will be going away for St Nikolaas.'

'But I can't...'

The porter had returned with the wheelchair and Britannia was whisked into it, had her hand shaken once more by the genial Doctor Berens and was wheeled away while she was still gathering her wits. It wasn't until she had been settled in the car once more, and the professor was driving through the city, that she said again: 'I can't...'

Her companion's voice was silky. 'If you do not like the idea of staying under my roof, Britannia, I must point out that the house is large enough to shelter the pair of us with little risk of meeting.'

'Oh, no—it's not that at all. But if I stay with you I'm—I'm a continuing source of embarrassment to you.'

His surprise was quite genuine. 'Why on earth should you be?' he wanted to know. 'We shan't be on our own, you know. It is December—or had you overlooked that? My sisters, their husbands and children, not to mention nursemaids, my mother, an un-

cle or two and—er—Madeleine will be celebrating
St Nikolaas with me.'

Put like that it made her feel lonely. 'You're very
kind, but won't I be a nuisance?'

His careless: 'Lord, no—I'll get a nurse to look
after you,' was really all she needed to round off a
horrid morning, but she wasn't going to let it show.
'You will be good enough to let me have the bill
for her fees,' she said haughtily, 'and I should like
to be home—among my friends and family—for
Christmas.'

'Long before that, I hope,' he assured her with
offhand cheerfulness, 'and it is your fault, if I may
say so, Britannia, that you're not in the bosom of
my family for St Nikolaas—but you turned me
down, if you care to remember.'

Britannia's bosom heaved under the ample folds
of Mevrouw Veske's anorak. 'You're quite awful!'
she snapped. 'I didn't turn you down—at least, it
was because...you know why it was.' She drew a
deep breath. 'Couldn't I please go home?'

'No. Not unless you don't mind having giddy fits
and falling down and spraining the other ankle.'

They had been travelling fast, now he slowed to
turn into the drive. 'Mevrouw Veske is coming to
see you this afternoon, she will bring your things
with her. If you can bear to take my advice I suggest
that you stay in bed for the rest of today. Emmie

will look after you and I'll bring a nurse back with me this evening.'

Britannia bit her lip; she had no arguments left and now her head was beginning to ache. She said, 'Thank you, Professor,' in a meek voice, and when he reminded her: 'Jake,' repeated 'Jake,' just as meekly.

Mevrouw Veske came after lunch, escorted to Britannia's room by Mevrouw Luitingh van Thien. She was cosily sympathetic, and full of motherly advice and barely concealed excitement, because here was Britannia, as lovely and sweet a girl as she had ever set eyes on, and moreover, she felt sure, as lovely and sweet a girl as the professor had ever set eyes on too, actually guest in his house, and likely to stay for a few days at least.

She embraced Britannia gingerly with an anxious eye on the bruise, and began to voice her regrets about St Nikolaas: 'All arranged weeks ago, you understand, my dear,' she protested, 'otherwise we would have loved to have had you with us…'

'Your loss is our gain, *mevrouw*,' interposed Mevrouw Luitingh van Thien. 'We shall be delighted to have Britannia with us.'

'She will perhaps be confined to her room?'

'So I understand, but my son is bringing back a nurse this evening.'

Britannia, sitting up in her pretty bed between her

two visitors, thought that it was very evident that
however merry the celebrations were to be she was
to have no part in them. She said a little desperately:
'Look, surely I could travel? If someone could take
me to the plane...'

'Jake has said that you are to stay here, my dear.'
The two ladies looked at her in a kindly fashion,
each of them quite sure in her own way that Jake
was right. Britannia gave up, for the time being at
least; when the professor returned, she would have
another go at him.

But he gave her no opportunity of doing this; indeed, thinking about it afterwards, she suspected that
he had guessed her intention and made sure that she
was unable to carry it out, for he had visited her on
his return that evening but had stayed only long
enough to introduce Zuster Hagenbroek, examine
her bruises and ankle, assure her with cool sympathy
that no great harm had been done to her person, and
that she would be as right as a trivet in no time at
all, before going away again, leaving her to the min-
istrations of Zuster Hagenbroek, a middle-aged, bus-
tling person with a wide smile and kind eyes, who
spoke surprisingly good English, assured Britannia
that she was perfectly able to massage the offending
ankle as well as exercise it, and that Britannia would
be up and about before she knew where she was.

Precisely the same sentiments as the professor had voiced, but with a great deal more warmth.

The next day or two passed pleasantly enough, the pain was less now and although her face was all colours of the rainbow down one side from eye to chin, Britannia's headache had gone. She sat out of bed on a chaise longue before the fire, playing endless games of cards with Zuster Hagenbroek, writing reassuring letters to her mother and father, and sustaining lengthy visits from the professor's mother, who, now that she had got to know her better, proved not to be in the least severe.

Of the professor she saw very little and never alone, either he came when Zuster Hagenbroek was on duty, or was accompanied by his mother or Emmie, and even then he didn't stop long, confining his conversation to her state of health, the weather, and any instructions he might have for Zuster Hagenbroek. Just as though, thought Britannia sadly, they were strangers.

It was on the following morning, after a particularly pointless conversation with him which had led to an almost sleepless night on her part, that the first of the visitors arrived for St Nikolaas—the professor's eldest sister, Emma, a young woman of thirty-five or so, accompanied by three daughters ranging from twelve years to six. There was a very small son, too, already whisked away to the nursery by his

nanny: 'But you shall see him later,' said his proud
mother, 'though you mustn't let the children bother
you.'

She was very like her brother, tall and graceful
and elegant, and, unlike him, warmly friendly. They
were getting to know each other when another sister
arrived, to be introduced as Francesca. She had two
children, six and seven-year-olds, who shook Britannia's hand and exhibited endearing gap-toothed
grins before they were led away for their lunch. But
the mothers remained until Marinus brought drinks
upstairs, sitting around happily gossiping in their excellent English until Zuster Hagenbroek came in
with Britannia's tray. Eating the delicious little
meal, she reflected that perhaps St Nikolaas wasn't
going to be so bad after all. And for the rest of that
day it wasn't; the professor's youngest sister Corinne arrived before tea with a placid baby boy who
slept through the not inconsiderable noise which his
numerous cousins made. Dumped on Britannia's lap
while his mother went on some errand, he tucked
his head, with its wisps of pale hair, into her arm
and closed his eyes. He had, she thought, the faintest
resemblance to his uncle.

And presently the professor came home. Britannia, watching his sisters launch themselves at his
vast person with cries of delight, wished with all her
heart that he would look like that for her, laughing

and relaxed and content, but when he broke loose
at length and came across to where she lay on the
chaise-longue, and she looked hopefully up into his
face, it was to meet cold eyes and an unsmiling
mouth, although he asked her civilly enough if she
had had a pleasant day and how she did. Conscious
of three pairs of eyes upon them, she answered quietly that yes, her day had been pleasant, and she did
very well, adding a conventional hope that he had
had a good day at the hospital.

His 'So-so,' was laconic in the extreme.

She didn't see him for the rest of that evening,
although his sisters poked their heads round the door
from time to time, for there was a good deal of coming and going getting the children to bed, and when
the various husbands arrived just before dinner, they
were brought along to be introduced before everyone trooped downstairs to the dining room. But not
Britannia; she thought wistfully of the family party
downstairs and wished she were there too, but that
of course was impossible; dressing would have been
a bit of a problem, she reminded herself sensibly,
and then there was the question of getting someone
to carry her downstairs, and as no one had suggested
it, presumably no one had thought of it, either. She
ate her dinner in solitary state because Zuster Hagenbroek had the afternoon and evening free and
wouldn't be back until bedtime.

Emmie came to take her tray and ask her if she wanted anything, but she had all she wanted; books, magazines, a book of crossword puzzles to solve, cards for Patience, all arranged on the little table beside her. She played a game of Patience, cheating so that it came out, and then lay back with her eyes closed. She kept them closed when the door opened and someone came in because if they thought she was asleep they wouldn't feel guilty about not entertaining her. No one else came, not until Zuster Hagenbroek returned and that astute lady, taking one look at Britannia's lonely face, embarked on a description of her visit to her family in Arnhem, which lasted through the preparations for bed and until she put out the light, saying firmly that Britannia was tired and must go to sleep immediately. She sounded so sure that she would do as she was told that Britannia did just that.

The professor came the next morning after breakfast, examined the ankle and pronounced it to be mending well. 'I will take the strapping off tomorrow,' he promised, 'put on an elastic stocking and you can try a little—a very little, weight on it. Exercises and massage as usual today, and see that you rest it.' He gave her a pleasant nod, added a few instructions to Zuster Hagenbroek, and went off, leaving Britannia with a number of questions she wanted answered and hadn't even had the chance to ask. To get away as quickly as possible was her one wish; whatever the professor had felt for her had obviously been transitory, for now he treated her with the scrupulous politeness of a good host entertaining a guest he didn't really want. And she must be a great embarrassment to him too, and hadn't he said that Madeleine de Venz would be there for St Nikolaas? Britannia pondered her problems until a headache threatened and then was fortunately prevented from worrying any more for the moment by the arrival of the professor's sisters, wandering in in ones and twos, some with their children, all talking cheerfully about the evening's festivities.

The morning passed pleasantly, and Britannia, with the prospect of an equally pleasant afternoon, ate her lunch with appetite, submitted to Zuster Hagenbroek's massage and exercises and then obliged Corinne by minding the baby for a while while his mother went off to help organise the evening with her mother. He lay in the crook of her arm, smiling windily at her from time to time and making tiny chirruping noises, and presently fell asleep, and because she was afraid to disturb him by reaching for her book, she closed her eyes too.

It was Madeleine's voice which roused her from her doze. 'What a picture!' declared her sweet, high voice from the doorway. 'Mother and child—only of course Britannia isn't a mother—in any case she looks quite unsuitable for the role with that bruise.'

Britannia turned her head. The professor was standing there and so was Madeleine, elegant—breathtakingly so—in a red fox jacket and a suede skirt. She said 'Good afternoon,' politely and hated the professor for not reproving the girl for her rudeness. She barely glanced at him, but fixed her eyes on his top waistcoat button and said quietly: 'Please don't wake the baby.'

The professor spoke softly to his companion and Madeleine gave him a surprised look which turned to ill-humour. Britannia had no idea what it was she snapped in answer, but she turned on her heel and went and he came into the room.

'Corinne seems to be making use of you,' he observed mildly.

'She had to do something or other, and the other children are out in the grounds with the two nannies.'

He sat down cautiously on the chaise-longue beside her injured ankle, and said to surprise her: 'I'm sorry that Madeleine was rude—she's a highly strung girl and doesn't always choose her words. You didn't look very pleased to see us.' He grinned suddenly. 'Jealous of the fox jacket?'

Britannia wiped away a dribble on the baby's chin. 'What a silly question,' she said coldly. 'How could I be jealous of anyone who wears the skin of a trapped animal?' She added austerely: 'I hope you had a good day at the hospital.'

'You know, if you didn't ask me that each day when I get home, I should feel positively deprived. Yes, I had a good day. I'm home early because everyone in Holland who can get home does so on St Nikolaas. Zuster Hagenbroek will be going to the bosom of her family in half an hour or so; she will come back quite late, I expect.'

'I'm glad she can go home.' It was a pity she couldn't think of anything else to say; the conversation so far had hardly sparkled.

'And how will you manage?' he asked blandly.

'Very well. I'm perfectly able to look after myself.' She added with a rush: 'I'm well enough to go home, if you would be so kind as to arrange it.'

'All in good time, Britannia. You have enough to read? I daresay my sisters have called in on you...'

'Yes, thank you, and yes, they have. I enjoyed it.' She wouldn't look at him while she sought for something else to say. Since he appeared to have settled himself he could at least help the conversation along.

The little silence was broken by Corinne's whirlwind entry. 'You dear girl,' she exclaimed warmly, and: 'Hullo, Jake—here, take your nephew and give Britannia a rest.' She dumped her son in the professor's arms and sat down on a low chair by the fire. 'Well, we're all ready and the children are in such a state of excitement I should think they'll all be sick later on.' She glanced at them both. 'Having a nice chat, were you?' she asked. 'Did I interrupt something?'

The professor didn't bother to answer it, it was Britannia who said: 'No—we were only passing the time of day.'

'Oh, good. I told Emmie I'd have tea with you, Britannia, do you mind? I can't stand having to sit and listen to Madeleine dripping platitudes in that sugary voice.'

'I will not tolerate discourtesy towards my guests, Corinne,' observed the professor severely.

She made a face at him, got up and took her small son from him and tweaked her brother's imposing nose. 'You old humbug,' she said. 'I may be fifteen years younger than you, but I've got eyes in my head, you know. Are you going to the sitting room for tea?'

'You have never grown up, my dear, have you? No, I have some work to do.' He added with some force: 'And no remarks about that, if you please.'

He smiled at her, nodded to Britannia and went away, and Corinne, settling down in her chair again, remarked: 'He's an old dear, isn't he? Bad-tempered, of course, but then so was Father, and he hates to be bested, though I don't suppose anyone's ever succeeded in doing that; he's so clever, you see, and he knows just about everything, although he hasn't a clue how to manage his love life,' she added artlessly. Her blue eyes smiled into Britannia's. 'He's a super brother and he'll make a gorgeous husband to the right girl. Do you like Madeleine?'

'I don't know her.' Britannia had almost been caught off guard. 'She's very beautiful, isn't she?'

'So are you.'

Britannia pinkened a little. 'Thank you. Tell me, how is it that you all speak such wonderful English?'

'We had a nanny—a fierce old bird; and then we had a governess, and Father always made us speak English at meals, and Jake kept it up, and now we're all married and none of us have lost the habit. You don't speak any Dutch?'

Britannia shook her head. 'No—well, about six words, and if someone says something easy like "Are you cold?" very slowly, I can understand them. Otherwise it's hopeless.'

'You'll learn. Here's tea, and I'm famished.' Corinne handed Britannia the baby. 'Tuck him under your arm, will you, and I'll pour.'

Alone again after tea, Britannia lay listening to the distant small voices echoing up the staircase; there were a lot of children—she could imagine how

excited they must be, although she was a little uncertain as to what exactly was to happen. She had
been going to ask Zuster Hagenbroek, but that dear
soul had already gone and although Emmie had been
in once or twice to see if she wanted anything, her
Dutch just wasn't up to asking; even if it had, she
would never have understood.

But she was to find out. She was reading by the
light of the table lamp beside her when the professor
returned. 'The *Sint* arrives in ten minutes—do you
want to comb your hair or anything before I take
you downstairs?'

'Me? Downstairs? Why?'

'My dear good girl, you don't really imagine that
I—or anyone else for that matter—would leave you
sitting here alone when St Nikolaas comes to call?'

'I'm not dressed.'

His eyes swept over her pink woolly housecoat
with its ruffled neck and velvet trimming. 'You are
a good deal more dressed than most of the ladies
downstairs.' He walked over to the dressing-table
and came back with a hairbrush and a mirror. 'Here
you are. Where do you keep the things you put on
your face?'

She was studying her face, a normal size now but
still blue and yellow all down one side. 'I'm a fright.
They're in the bathroom, on the shelf.'

She brushed her hair and tied it back neatly, powdered her nose and applied lipstick. 'There, am I all right?'

He picked her up and started for the door. 'My darling girl, not only are you all right, you're quite breathtakingly beautiful.'

CHAPTER SEVEN

THE PROFESSOR'S REMARK, coming as it did after several days of coldness, so astonished Britannia that she stayed quiet as he took her downstairs and across the hall, this time not to the sitting room but down a wide passage at the side of the staircase, with doors on one side and a big arched door at its end. Outside this he paused, kissed her hard and swiftly and pushed the door open with his foot. The room was very large, with enormous windows with crimson curtains drawn across them to shut out the chilly dark evening. The floor was of polished wood with a great centre carpet and the furniture was satinwood, upholstered in shades of rose and cream and blue. Britannia, laid gently on to a sofa drawn up to one side of the great hearth, stared around her with great interest. It was a very grand room and the people in it looked grand too. The women had dressed for the occasion and she quite saw what Jake had meant when he said that she was more dressed than the other ladies present, for whereas she was muffled to the throat in cosy wool, they were in long evening gowns, beautiful garments such as she had often gazed at in Fortnum and Mason's windows or Harrods, and the men were in black ties to complement them. Very conscious of her prosaic appearance, she smiled rather shyly at Mevrouw Luitingh van Thien, who came across the room to sit beside her.

'My dear, how very nice that you can join us,' said that lady in a ringing voice. 'How pretty you look, and how I wish I had your lovely hair. You know everyone here, don't you? I must warn you that presently it will become very noisy and you are to say immediately if you get the headache.'

She patted Britannia's arm, her severe features lighted by a delightful smile. 'Jake's two uncles are here, you shall meet them presently, they are talking to Madeleine.'

Which gave Britannia the chance to look at her. Oyster crêpe, cut far too low for such a bony chest and too elaborate for the occasion. Quite unsuitable, almost as unsuitable as Britannia's own garment. She looked away quickly and met the smiling eyes of Corinne. 'We're going to sit near you, so that you will know what's happening. Jake has to be at the other end of the room to welcome the *Sint*. You see, we do it exactly the same every year, if we didn't the children would be disappointed. He's coming now.'

The big doors opened once more and the *Sint* entered, with Zwarte Piet behind him. The professor greeted him with a short speech and everybody

clapped while he walked, with the professor showing him the way, down the centre of the room to
where a space had been cleared for him and his attendant. He was an imposing figure in his crimson
and purple robes and his mitre set on a head with a
lavish display of white hair and beard. He carried a
book which Corinne whispered held the names of
all the children present. Provided they had been
good throughout the year, each child would receive
a present and an orange. Bad children were popped
into Zwarte Piet's sack, but this, Corinne concluded,
seldom happened.

Several of the children had come to sit on the sofa
with Britannia; now they were called one by one
and advanced to receive their gifts, so that there was
a good deal of paper being rustled and whispered
exclamations of delight going on around her. She
nodded and smiled and admired the boxes of paints,
dolls, clockwork engines and the like which quickly
strewed the sofa, and was busy tying a doll's bonnet
more securely when she became aware that the children had given way to the grownups. And certainly
the good *Sint* had been generous; Corinne waltzed
up to the good man, received her gift, kissed him
for it amidst a good deal of laughter, and returned
to the sofa to open it; earrings, quite beautiful ones
of sapphires and pearls—antique and very valuable,
thought Britannia, and then turned to admire Mev-

rouw Luitingh van Thien's gift, a thick gold chain with a locket and quite lovely. Everyone else had something similar too, although she was relieved to see that Madeleine's present—an evening bag—had a less personal flavour. She was quite taken by surprise when her own name was called and the professor said: 'I'll take it for you, Britannia. St Nikolaas has it from me that you have been a good girl and deserve your gift.'

He brought it over presently and she thanked him in a quiet little voice and undid the beribboned package. It was a headscarf, a Gucci, pink and brown and cream and a hint of green, a lovely thing. She wondered who had bought it and the professor, who hadn't gone away, bent and whispered in her ear just as though she had asked him. 'I hope you like it, the colours reminded me of you.'

She thanked him again and this time when she looked at him, his eyes were warm and he was smiling, so that she smiled too. She wasn't sure what she might have said next if Madeleine hadn't joined the little group round them, slipped a hand under the professor's arm and made some laughing remark about her present. 'And just the colour I wanted,' she went on. 'So clever of you, Jake dear, to choose it.' She smiled down at Britannia. 'That's a charming scarf—I don't suppose you have ever had a Gucci before.'

'No.' The sight of Madeleine's hand on Jake's arm, just as though it belonged there, made Britannia uncertain. 'I shall love wearing it.'

Emma had joined them too; she began to talk to Britannia almost immediately and Britannia didn't see Jake and Madeleine go away. The party began to split up into groups and the children made a dutiful round of goodnights. They had sung themselves hoarse as St Nikolaas had made his dignified way out of the room once more, they had drunk their lemonade and eaten their *speculaas* and as much of their chocolate letters as they had been allowed, now they were more than ready for bed. The room seemed larger than ever once they had gone, but very pleasant in the glow of the many rose-coloured lamps and the firelight. Presently Marinus came in with drinks and Britannia was just beginning to worry as to how she was to get back upstairs again when the professor returned, picked her up and carried her across the hall and into the dining room, where he sat her on a chair at one corner of the great rectangular table, her leg on a cushioned stool.

'Oh, but I can't,' she protested. 'It's a family dinner party—and I'm not dressed.'

'You've said that already. Here's Corinne's husband to sit beside you and Oom Jiers, and if you think that a strange name, he's from Friesland.'

He left her with her two table companions and

went to the head of the table at the farther end so that she couldn't really see him very well unless she peered round Oom Jiers' considerable bulk. It was small comfort that Madeleine was seated quite close to him, near enough to talk to him if she wanted to. Britannia decided not to spoil her dinner by trying to see what he was doing and applied herself to Corinne's husband, Jan, and then to Oom Jiers, who proved to be a man of wit despite his elderly appearance.

They settled down to enjoy themselves. As Jan said, there was nothing like good conversation and good food to go with it, and it was certainly that; lobster soup, rich and creamy, followed by roast leg of pork with spiced peaches, served on a great silver dish and carved, suitably, by the professor amid a good deal of joking from his family, and as well as the peaches there were dishes of vegetables, handed round by Marinus and the two maids. Britannia, doing justice to her dinner, found it all the better by reason of the exquisite china upon which it was served and the rat-tailed silver spoons and forks, worn thin with use but as lovely as the day they had first been used some time in the seventeenth century.

The sweet was sheer luxury; mangoes in champagne, served in exquisite wine glasses, and they drank champagne too, so that by the end of the meal Britannia was feeling a good deal happier than she had done. All the same, as soon as they had had coffee she decided that she would make some excuse and go back to her room; it was, after all, a family gathering and although everyone—well, nearly everyone—had been very sweet to her, she was conscious of feeling an outsider. She had her opportunity quite soon, for the professor wandered round the table as they all got up to go back to the sitting room, with the obvious intention of carrying her there.

She didn't give him a chance to speak but said at once: 'I've had a simply lovely time, but I'd like to go upstairs now, if you wouldn't mind.'

'I mind very much, Britannia.' He made no attempt to lower his voice and she was painfully aware that Jan and Oom Jiers were both listening quite openly; not only that, Madeleine, from the other side of the table, was watching them.

'I think I'm tired,' she elaborated.

He smiled then, a tender little smile which was just for her but which must have been seen by anyone who happened to be looking. 'Shall we compromise? Don't go to your room just yet, we will go to the little sitting room my mother sometimes uses, and sit quietly and talk.'

She supposed that it was the champagne that made his suggestion sound so delightful, but all the same she asked: 'But your guests? You can't leave them.'

'Oom Jiers will fill in for me, won't you? And they're not guests—they're family.'

She eyed him steadily, not caring now that their two companions were drinking in every word. 'Madeleine isn't family—or is she, Jake?'

'You are a persistent young woman, Britannia. No, she isn't family, but I—we have all known her for a very long time, she has come to our St Nikolaas feast for years.' He added in a slightly louder voice: 'Of course, if you prefer, I'll take you to your room, we can talk there just as easily.'

It was the professor's mother who clinched the matter. 'Of course you can't leave us now, my dear. Why not let Jake take you to the little sitting room for a while? It will be quiet there and when you feel rested you can come back and join us.'

Britannia hadn't seen her join them, she had no idea how long the lady had been standing there but in any event, she didn't seem to mind. She looked across the table and saw Madeleine's face. If it had been unhappy she wouldn't have agreed, but it wasn't, it was furious, the lovely eyes narrowed, the mouth a thin line. 'All right,' she said, 'I think I should like to do that, if it's not being a nuisance.'

So she was carried once more across the hall and through a small arched door on the other side of it, to a much smaller room, but still large by her own home standards. She guessed that it was in the older part of the house, for the windows were narrow and latticed and the fireplace was an open one with a great copper hood above it. The professor set her down on a narrow Regency sofa drawn up to the hearth, turned off the wall sconces leaving only a couple of rose-shaded table lamps burning, and sat down in a winged armchair opposite her. 'We all love this room,' he remarked pleasantly. 'Mama used it a great deal when we were children, we used to come and talk to her here while she sat and sewed. When my father came home he would come straight here.'

'Was he a surgeon too?'

'Oh, yes, and his father before him. He died ten years ago, he was a good deal older than my mother.'

Britannia looked around her, more at ease now because the professor had apparently forgotten that he had called her his darling girl and kissed her into the bargain. The room was charming and she liked the furniture—applewood and walnut and a golden mahogany and some delicate pieces of marquetry, all welded into a charming whole by the deep red and blue patterned curtains and covers. 'It's delightful. You have a very beautiful house, Jake.' She sighed without knowing it. 'Sitting here and sew-ing...'

'I shall do exactly the same as my father.' She gave him an enquiring look, and he went on: 'Come straight to you here when I get home each evening.'

Britannia went pink; he was joking and it hurt, but she said austerely: 'If you brought me here to make jokes like that, then I'd like to go back to my room, please.'

'I brought you here to ask you, in peace and quiet, to marry me, Britannia.' He was still sitting back in his great chair, relaxed and calm and she jerked up-right the better to stare at him. The sudden move-ment hurt her ankle and she winced, and he was at once beside her, rearranging the cushion.

'You seem surprised,' he observed mildly. 'Surely you must have expected me to do just that.'

Britannia said indignantly: 'Of course I'm sur-prised! If it hadn't been for this silly ankle I should have been back in England and how could you have—have asked me to marry you then?'

'Easily enough, although the journey would have been tiresome, my dear.'

'Yes, but I explained—I mean, about Made-leine...you said...'

'You said, darling Britannia—you had a good deal to say, I have never met such a girl for giving her opinion about this, that and the other.'

She kept doggedly to the point. 'But she's here, in your house, you—invited her.'

'To be honest, I did not. You must understand that for a number of years Madeleine has been spending St Nikolaas with us, it has become a kind of habit, and one can hardly say: "Well, Madeleine, we don't want you to come any more," can one? She has, over the last year or so, taken it for granted just as, I'm afraid, it was taken for granted that sooner or later I should ask her to marry me.'

'She still takes it for granted.'

'Oh, I think not; I have never asked her to do so, you know, and she must surely realise by now that I have no intention of doing so.'

Britannia looked at him lovingly. Men were a bit foolish sometimes, even a man like Jake, self-assured and brilliantly clever and knowing what he wanted, casually taking it for granted that Madeleine would give way with good grace to a girl he hardly knew...'You seem very certain of me,' she remarked with faint tartness.

He raised his eyebrows. 'But of course I am; you may preach at me and take me to task on every possible occasion, but you love me, don't you?'

'Yes,' said Britannia, baldly, and was instantly joined on her sofa by the professor, who put an arm around her and observed with satisfaction: 'That's better.' He kissed the top of her head. 'Now let us be sensible and assess the situation.' He paused: 'Well, let us be sensible presently.' He put the other arm around her and bent to kiss her, an exercise which took quite a time and which Britannia didn't attempt to interrupt. After a little while he said: 'How soon can you leave the hospital?'

Britannia lifted her head from his shoulder, the better to concentrate on her arithmetic. 'Well, let me see, today's the fifth of December, so a month away is the second of January, but I've got three weeks' holiday owing, so I'd have a week to do plus sick leave to make up...'

'Far too long—you'll allow me to deal with it for you. I think it would be nice if we got married before Christmas.'

She lifted her head once more to look at him. 'Jake—that's three weeks away!'

'Too long. Do you want to be married here or in England?'

She said instantly: 'At home, please. Jake, you're rushing me...'

His arm tightened. 'Yes, I know I am, but I won't if you don't want me to.'

She leaned up to kiss his chin. 'You're really very nice when one gets to know you. I want time to get used to it all, Jake. Would you mind very much if we don't make any plans for a few days—a week? Then I'll do anything you say, I promise you. I'd like to tell my parents, you see they know about you, I—I told them how we met…'

'Ah, so you knew, too.'

'Oh, yes, but I didn't think I'd see you again.'

The professor laughed gently. 'You forget that I knew where you were, my darling. I had every intention of seeing you again.'

'You said I had a sharp tongue.'

'And so you have on occasion, my love, but it doesn't worry me in the least, I quite enjoy it.' There was a pleasant little interlude while he proved this statement, but presently Britannia said: 'We ought to go back. I'd like to stay here with you for the rest of the evening, but it wouldn't do.'

The professor looked as though he was going to laugh, although he agreed quite seriously to this. 'But I shall carry you back to your room in half an hour or so. Emmie will help you get ready for bed. Is your ankle quite all right? We'll have that strapping off tomorrow—I'll come home after the morning list and see to it—you can try a little weight bearing once it's off and the stocking is on. You'll be walking quite soon provided you're sensible about resting it.'

He picked her up and carried her back to the sitting room, and just as he had done earlier in the evening, bent to kiss her before he opened the door.

She was settled on the sofa by the fire once more

and Jake went away again, to reappear presently
with Marinus bearing a large tray with glasses, and
Emmie behind him with a magnum of champagne
in a silver bucket. Marinus put the tray down and
went back again for a second bottle and Emmie
reappeared with another tray loaded with small
dishes of petits fours and canapés. A toast was drunk
to St Nikolaas, someone went over to the grand piano at one end of the room and began to play and
presently everyone was singing the traditional songs
of the Feast of St Nikolaas, and Britannia, unable to
understand any of them, nonetheless picked up the
tunes and joined in, greatly helped by the champagne. Not even the sight of Madeleine crossing the
room to sit beside Jake could shake her happiness.
Poor Madeleine, imagining that she would marry
him. Britannia, disliking the girl very much, all the
same felt sorry for her.

The professor got up presently and came over to
the sofa, reminded her that she was to go to bed,
waited while she wished everyone a good night and
carried her upstairs, calling to Corinne on his way
to go with them, and once in her room he laid Britannia on her bed, kissed her gently on the cheek,
wished her goodnight and went away immediately,
leaving Corinne looking delighted and curious.

'I suppose it is one of those open secrets everyone

knows,' she declared happily, 'you and Jake. When are you going to announce it?'

Britannia was wriggling out of her dressing gown. 'However did you know?'

Corinne giggled. 'I don't think I exactly knew, none of us did, but we guessed. Mother's so happy about it, so are we all.'

Britannia felt a delightful wave of happiness wash over her. 'How nice of you—only Madeleine…'

'She hasn't guessed. She's so conceited and sure of Jake that she can't imagine him falling in love with anyone but her.' Corinne sat down on the edge of the bed. 'None of us likes her, she wormed her way in and she was very clever, always good company for Jake and always at the same houses and parties and dinners…she was always there, you see, creeping into his life until he took her for granted.'

'Go on,' urged Britannia, and was disappointed when Emmie came in, taking charge with all the firmness of a trusted old servant, so that Corinne went obediently away and left her to help Britannia to bed.

But Britannia was too happy to lie awake worrying about Madeleine; she slept soundly on the thought that Jake loved her and they were going to marry very soon. This pleasant glow continued throughout the morning, and although no one actually asked her any questions, there was a good deal

of family discussion in which she was included as
though she were already one of them, and when after
lunch Jake came home, he came straight to her room
and with Zuster Hagenbroek's assistance, took the
strapping off the ankle, examined it at length, en-
cased it in an elastic stocking pronounced it well on
the way to recovery and declared that he would be
back in half an hour, during which time she could
dress. 'A stick and a strong arm is what you need
now, we'll try them out presently.' He looked at
Zuster Hagenbroek. 'I think we can manage without
you after today—if you can be ready, I'll run you
in after breakfast tomorrow.'

He went away, and Britannia got down to the
business of dressing while Zuster Hagenbroek tidied
the room and gossiped. She had heard about Britannia and the professor, she said happily, the whole
household knew, and everyone was so pleased. She
stopped to smile broadly at Britannia. Such a nice
man he was too, very popular at the hospital and
with an enormous private practice, but perhaps Britannia knew about that? And no puffed-up airs and
graces, either, for all he was a wealthy man, but of
course that wasn't news... And when, asked the dear
soul, was the wedding to be?

Britannia said that she didn't know; nothing had
been decided, but it would be a very quiet one. 'And
I hope that when I'm settled in you'll come and see

me, for you've been so kind—I don't know what I should have done without you.'

Zuster Hagenbroek looked gratified. 'Well, you've been a model patient—and here's the professor back again.'

Britannia had done her face with extra care and brushed her hair until it shone. She had put on a tweed skirt and a pink woolly sweater which she knew suited her very well and now she turned to the door, her face alight with happiness as the professor came in. 'Are you home for the rest of the day?' she wanted to know.

'I must go back to my rooms for an hour this evening—I've a couple of patients I have to see, but I'll be back for dinner. How's the ankle?'

'Fine.' She felt a little shy of him because this was the Jake she didn't know very well, the calm, rather impersonal surgeon—not that she would have liked him to have been anything else while Zuster Hagenbroek was there.

He carried her downstairs, set her on a high-backed chair in the hall and fetched a stick from the wall cupboard. 'I thought you might like to see over some of the house, darling. We won't hurry and you can sit down every now and then, I know you've been in the sitting room and the big drawing room, but there are some quite interesting paintings and the silver is worth looking at too.'

He came over to her and pulled her gently to her feet and stood looking down at her, laughing. 'Why do you look like that? Are you shy?'

She shook her head. 'No, at least, only a little. You see, I don't know you very well…'

'My darling, but you do. The number of times you have pointed out my faults and given me advice as to how to overcome them…'

She stood within the circle of his arm. 'I always thought you were such a bad-tempered man…'

'I am, but not at the moment.' He kissed her again. 'Let's start in the sitting room, shall we? We're bound to meet the family, but we won't let them hinder us.'

The afternoon was a delight to her; she had a natural flair for beautiful things and some of the portraits on the walls were beautiful, as were the silver and the porcelain in their great marquetry cabinets. They spent a long time in the sitting room before they inspected the dining room, the big drawing room, and a charming smaller room which was the little drawing room, with white-painted walls and soft pink and blue furnishings, little inlaid tables and a collection of watercolours hung on either side of the steel fireplace. Jake pointed out a Leickert, a van Schendel and a van der Stok which an ancestor had commissioned in the nineteenth century, and over and above those were a Carabain and two charming river scenes by van Deventer which he had bought during the last few years.

'We shall be able to search for treasures together,' he observed, and stopped to kiss her before picking her up and carrying her down a small staircase. 'This is the oldest part of the house and on a different level. There's a games room and a garden room and here at the end is the music room. Do you play the piano, Britannia?'

She hobbled to the baby grand piano in the big bay window. 'A little.' She ran her fingers up and down the yellowed keys and then sat down on the wide stool and tried a little Chopin. She played with spirit if a bit inaccurately, but she stopped when Jake sat down beside her and took over the tune.

'No, go on, my love—I come here sometimes for half an hour, now we can share an added pleasure!'

He played well and with no tiresome mannerisms; they thundered through a mazurka and then skimmed through a waltz, and when they stopped Britannia said: 'Jake, you play very well—I had no idea…'

He gave her a wicked glance. 'We shall probably have a child prodigy.'

'Oh, no,' cried Britannia, 'not a musician, they'll all be brilliant surgeons like their papa.'

'So I am to be rivalled in my old age?'

She answered him seriously. 'Not rivalled, for

you will have handed on your skill, just as your father did to you. And you'll never be old.'

'My darling, there is fifteen years' difference between us.' He had closed the piano and was leaning on it, looking at her with a little mocking smile.

'Pooh, what's fifteen years,' cried Britannia with some asperity, and then suddenly: 'You don't think it's too much? You don't think that I... Jake, perhaps after we're married you'll wish we weren't. You don't know much about me and nothing of my family, would it be better if we waited?'

'You have second thoughts?' His voice was faintly cool and she hastened to protest.

'Of course I haven't, not for me.' She frowned a little. 'I think what it is, I wanted to marry you so much and now I'm going to and it doesn't seem possible, it's like a lovely dream and I'm afraid of waking up.'

'Then I must convince you that you are wrong.' Which he did to such good purpose that Britannia forgot all her doubts and kissed him back.

The garden room was full of colour even on the grey winter's afternoon; they wandered around while Britannia admired the chrysanthemums and the forced spring flowers and an enormous assortment of house plants.

'But it's one person's work,' observed Britannia.

'More or less—old Cor sees to this side of the

greenhouses. When you can manage it, we'll go and look at the gardens and the hothouses. Shall we join the family for tea, or would you like it here?'

'They're all going tomorrow, aren't they? and they haven't seen much of you.' She would have liked to have stayed there alone with Jake, but it might look as though she wasn't prepared to share him with his family. They went slowly through the house again and into the sitting room, full of people. The children were there too, the little ones under the wing of the two nannies, the babies on any lap which came handy, while everyone talked their heads off. Britannia, settled on a sofa with her foot up once more, was instantly absorbed into the cheerful gathering and now they spoke quite openly about her joining the family, laughingly warning her that New Year would be a splendid opportunity for her to meet even more of them. 'You'll have to open up all the bedrooms, Britannia, there are hordes of us; Emmie cooks for days before and Jake gives a dance; it's tremendous fun.'

Britannia suppressed a tiny qualm; supposing she couldn't cope with entertaining on that scale? There would be any number of things she wouldn't know, and would Jake expect her to know them? Just for a moment she thought of Madeleine, who would know exactly what to do on such an occasion and be relied upon to be a perfect hostess. And suppos-

ing she did something silly and Jake felt ashamed
of her? She looked up and found the professor's eye
on her and he shook his head slightly at her and
smiled, just as though he guessed what she was
thinking.

He took her with him the next afternoon; he had
patients to see at his consulting rooms and as he
explained, it would be a good opportunity for her to
see them and meet Mien, his secretary, and Willa,
the receptionist and nurse. There were his two part-
ners whom she must meet, too, he told her, but not
just yet; one was on holiday, the other in Luxem-
bourg. So Britannia, wrapped up against the cold
wind and the fine powdering of snow which had
begun to fall, was made comfortable beside him
when he came to fetch her after lunch.

'Warm enough?' he wanted to know, sending the
car towards Arnhem. And when she nodded, for who
wouldn't be warm in such a magnificent car? he
went on: 'I should like to wrap you in furs, my darling, but I think that you wouldn't like that—not just
yet.'

He manoeuvred the car past a string of air force
jeeps. 'I haven't given you a ring, have I? But a ring
is binding.'

Britannia didn't know why his words should
make her suddenly cold inside; after all, she had
asked him to wait. She peeped sideways at him and

saw that his profile was stern. She said meekly: 'Yes, it is, isn't it?' and when he didn't say anything else she forbore from further speech. But when he drew up before one of the tall, narrow houses in a quiet side street of the city, the face he turned to her was quite free from any sternness.

'Wait while I get you out,' he cautioned, 'and I shall have to carry you up the stairs—there's a lift, but it's out of order.'

His rooms were on the first floor, indeed they occupied the whole of it, three consulting rooms, a most comfortably furnished waiting room, a tiny office for Mien, a bespectacled, rather plain girl with a charming smile, and another small room used by Willa for any small treatment which might be necessary. Britannia was enchanted by it all and spent the ensuing hours sitting with Mien, whose English was really rather good, while Jake went away to see his patients.

'It is a large practice,' explained Mien, 'and as well as his work here, the professor has many beds in the hospitals. He operates several times a week and also goes to Utrecht and to London and sometimes Vienna.'

And Britannia, anxious to know all there was to know about Jake, listened to every word. There was still so much to discover about him and not a great deal of time before they married. With Mien on the telephone beside her, Britannia went into a pleasant daydream; being married to Jake was going to be fun.

CHAPTER EIGHT

THE OLD HOUSE seemed very quiet after everyone had gone the next day, leaving only Mevrouw Luitingh van Thien behind. The professor had left before breakfast and it was after that meal that his mother suggested that she might take Britannia over the rest of the house. 'That's if you can manage the stairs, my dear,' she added. 'Jake would not forgive me if I suggested anything which might harm your ankle.'

'I can hop,' declared Britannia cheerfully. 'It's much better, you know, and the elastic stocking supports it. I'd love to come with you.'

Their tour took most of the morning, there was so much to see: magnificent bedrooms furnished with what Britannia could see were valuable antiques, cunningly concealed bathrooms and clothes closets and a dear little room which had been called 'Mevrouw's kamertje', a name which had been handed down from one generation to another without anyone really knowing why it should be so. It had a work table, its original silk lining still intact, though faded, and some small high-backed chairs which her guide assured her were most comfortable.

There was a games table too, exquisitely inlaid with applewood, and a sofa table in the window, as well as an escritoire with its accompanying chair. The curtains were brocade in muted greens and blues and the highly polished wood floor had a scattering of fine rugs upon it. The only concession to modernity were the table lamps; little silver stands with peach shades which blended exactly with the room.

They sat there for a little while carrying on a placid conversation about nothing in particular until Mevrouw Luitingh van Thien remarked unexpectedly: 'I have said nothing to you as yet, my dear, for Jake has told me that you want a few days in which to think over his proposal—indeed, he tells me that nothing has actually been settled, but I hope very much that you will accept him. I do not mind telling you now that I—in fact, all of us, have been very much against him marrying Madeleine de Venz.' She sighed. 'Not that he would have taken any notice of anything we might have had to say. You can imagine my delight, Britannia, when after years of dreaded expectation that he would marry her, he should meet you and fall in love with you at your first meeting.'

'He intended to marry her.' Britannia wasn't asking a question but stating a fact.

Her companion corrected her, 'No, my dear, she intended to marry him.'

Which remark merely substantiated what Britannia herself already knew. She picked up a dainty little figurine, admiring its vivid blue glaze and then looked at its base. 'Longton Hall,' she said absentmindedly, 'mid-eighteenth century and quite charming. Madeleine hates me.'

'Naturally, Britannia. You're not afraid of her?'

'Goodness me, no, *mevrouw*, not of her. She has become a habit with Jake—habits are hard to shake off. She has a lot that I haven't—breeding and knowing how to do things and what to say, she knows all his friends and, I daresay, how he likes his house run...'

Mevrouw Luitingh van Thien snorted elegantly. 'His servants dislike her, did you know that? Even the dogs avoid her.' She glanced round at the two faithful beasts who had accompanied them silently and were now sitting between them. 'And as for breeding, Britannia, I find your manners much more to my taste. She is sophisticated, certainly and probably able to cope with any social occasion, but there is no warmth in her; her love for Jake, if one can call it love, is purely selfish; if he were to lose his possessions overnight or fall victim to some incurable illness, she would have no more to do with him. You, I know, would love Jake under any circumstance.'

'Yes, I would,' said Britannia baldly. 'I'd starve

for him. And if I thought I wouldn't make him happy, then I'd go away.'

She frowned, for she hadn't meant to be quite so dramatic about it; one's thoughts sometimes sounded silly spoken aloud. But apparently Mevrouw Luitingh van Thien didn't think so; she said approvingly, 'I have always been sure of that, my dear.'

They sat in a comfortable silence for a few minutes and then went on with their inspection: the remainder of the bedroom on the first floor, and at the back of the house, in the older part, the large nursery, very much as it must have looked when the professor was a small boy; there was a night nursery too, and a bathroom and tiny kitchen and several smaller bedrooms. They inspected it in silence until Mevrouw Luitingh van Thien remarked softly: 'Jake's nanny married when Corinne left the nursery—she has a daughter who is also a nanny—a pleasant homely girl, like her mother.'

Britannia went a bright pink, but spoke up in her honest way. 'You mean she would come to us if we wanted her.'

'Yes, my dear, that is what I meant. We had better go back the way we came; there is a small staircase at the end of this passage, but it is too narrow for you. We will leave the top floor until you can walk in comfort. There is a wonderful view from the parapet and when the children were young, we turned one of the rooms into a games room where they could play those noisy games young people love. The other rooms are for the servants—they have a sitting room there too, and Emmie and Marinus have a small flat, and there are the attics, of course, full of the odds and ends families accumulate over the years.'

They were making their way back as she talked and now Britannia was making her way clumsily down the staircase. At the bottom she said politely: 'Thank you for showing me round; it's quite beautiful. Would you mind if I put my leg up for half an hour before lunch? It's a little uncomfortable.'

Which it was, but she wanted a little time to think, too. At the back of her mind she was worrying about Madeleine. She couldn't believe that she wouldn't do all she could to get Jake back, if she had ever had him... Britannia lay back on the sofa, determined to be sensible about it, think the whole thing out in a rational manner and make up her mind what to do. She didn't get very far, of course; she knew what she wanted to do; she wanted to marry Jake and when he brought the subject up again, she would tell him that. Having settled everything in this simple fashion, she closed her eyes and went to sleep.

The professor came home after lunch, examined

her ankle and pronounced it to be progressing splendidly, then suggested that they might drive to the outskirts of Hilversum and visit a friend of his, Reilof van Meerum. 'He has an English wife, Laura—I think you might like each other.'

'Don't you have any more patients today?'

'Lord, yes, but not until half past six at my rooms—I'll have to go on to the hospital after that to take a look at one of my patients there, but I'm free this afternoon. Like to come?'

Of course she liked to go with him. Madeleine was forgotten, she put on her outdoor things and limped downstairs under his watchful eye. 'You're making astounding progress,' he observed, 'but go easy on the stairs, my darling, and use a stick for another day or two.'

It was a cold, crisp day and the road to Apeldoorn was beautiful in the thin sunshine. Britannia occupied the few miles before they joined the motorway in telling Jake about her morning, and they passed the time pleasantly enough as they raced towards Amersfoort, and if she was a little disappointed because he had nothing to say concerning their future, she was careful not to let it spoil her happy mood. They left the motorway at Amersfoort and took the road to Baarn, and a mile or two beyond that pleasant town, along a fine avenue lined with great trees, he turned in between brick pillars and along a short drive, to stop before a large square house with a stone balustrade and a massive porch.

As Jake helped her out, Britannia asked: 'Are they expecting us?'

'I saw Reilof this morning and we are expected, my love.'

As if to substantiate his remark the door was flung open and a smallish girl with mousy hair and pretty eyes ran out. 'Reilof said you would be coming—what a lovely surprise.' She put up her face for Jake's kiss and turned to Britannia. 'I'm Laura,' she said. 'Reilof and Jake are old friends and I hope we'll be friends too.' She smiled and instantly looked pretty. 'Come in—Reilof's in the sitting room, guarding the twins—Nanny's got a day off.'

She led them indoors, where a white-haired man took their coats and exchanged a few dignified remarks with Jake and was made known to Britannia as Piet, without whom, Laura declared, the house would fall apart. 'We're in the small sitting room.'

Reilof van Meerum was standing by the window, a very small baby over his shoulder. The baby was making a considerable noise, but his proud parent was quite unruffled by it. He came forward to meet his visitors, shook Jake's hand as though he hadn't seen him in weeks and then turned to Britannia. 'Jake and I are such old friends that I don't suppose he'll mind if I kiss you.' He grinned. 'He always kisses Laura.' He glanced at his small wife with such devotion that Britannia caught her breath and then smiled as he went on. 'We're fearful bores at present, you know—we've only had the twins a month, and our days revolve round them.'

Britannia took a look at the baby on his arm; dark like his father and at the moment, very ill-tempered. The other baby, sleeping peacefully in its cradle, was dark too. 'A girl?' essayed Britannia, and Laura nodded. 'Yes—isn't it nice having one of each? She's called Beatrix Laura, and he's Reilof, of course.'

Reilof junior stopped screaming presently and was put to sleep in his cradle and the two men wandered off to Reilof's study while the two girls settled down for a gossip. There was a lot to talk about, as they had much in common, for Laura had been a nurse before she married Reilof. It wasn't until Piet had been in with the tea tray and gone to fetch his master that Laura asked diffidently: 'I'm not being nosey, but are you and Jake going to get married?'

'Yes,' Britannia told her, 'I hope so. But there's nothing definite yet.'

There was no time to do more than exchange smiles, for the two men came into the room then and the rest of the visit was taken up with light-hearted conversation. They left presently and started their journey back to Hoenderloo, travelling fast because Jake hadn't much time; perhaps it was because of that he had little to say in answer to Britannia's cheerful remarks about their afternoon, and when she took a quick peep at him it was to see that he was deep in thought, his mouth set sternly, and a faint frown between his eyes, so that her efforts at conversation dwindled away into silence. Something was annoying him—was still annoying him. At last, unable to bear the silence any longer, she said forthrightly: 'You look vexed. Have I done something?'

They were travelling very fast and he didn't look at her. 'No.' And then: 'I'm glad you enjoyed your afternoon.' But it was uttered in such an absent-minded fashion that she knew that he wasn't really thinking about that at all.

She didn't say any more then until they had reached the house once more and he had helped her out of the car and they were indoors, and although he was as kind and considerate as he always was towards her she sensed his impatience. 'I've a mind to climb the staircase by myself,' she told him lightly, 'and it's a good chance, because you want to be off again, don't you?'

She didn't wait for his reply but started off across the hall, walking quite firmly with her stick so that he would be able to see that she was independent now. But when she heard his footsteps cross the hall towards his study she paused thankfully to lean on the carved banisters before mounting the wide stairs. Jake had forgotten to shut the study door, she thought idly, and then froze as she heard the faint tinkle of the telephone as he lifted the receiver and said: 'Madeleine? *Ik moet met je spreken—morgen middag—zal je thuis wezen?*'

He spoke clearly and Britannia, who had picked up a little Dutch by now, understood him very well. He wanted to speak to Madeleine the following afternoon and would she be home. She started up the staircase while she pondered the unwelcome thought that possibly it had something to do with his ill-humour in the car. It took her a few minutes to dismiss the idea as nonsense; he had every right to telephone whom he wished and just because it had been Madeleine there was no reason for her to feel as she did—coldly apprehensive. It hadn't been such a good day after all, she decided as she took off her outdoor things and did her hair and face. Perhaps he had had an extra busy day and hadn't really wanted to go to see his friends. She went downstairs again to find him gone and his mother sitting by the fire, looking so normal that Britannia called herself an imaginative fool and embarked on a cheerful account of the afternoon. Everything, she told herself, would be all right when Jake got home later on.

Only he didn't come. There was a message just before they sat down for dinner to say that he had an emergency operation that evening and would get something to eat in hospital, and although Britannia sat up long after Mevrouw Luitingh van Thien had gone to bed, he didn't come, so presently she too went to bed, to lie awake and listen for the car. She slept in the end without hearing its return in the early hours of the morning.

She was surprised and pleased to find him at the breakfast table the next morning, and then not quite so pleased to see that he was still in a thoughtful mood; something was on his mind and she longed to ask him what. Instead she wished him a cheerful good morning, hoped that he hadn't had too busy an evening and asked if he was going to the hospital that morning.

He glanced up from the letter he was reading. 'Yes, and I don't expect to be home until after tea. Have you any plans for today? Don't, I beg of you, over-exercise that ankle. It's made a very rapid recovery, it would be a shame to spoil it.'

She waited for him to say something else; something about their future. Perhaps that was why he was so preoccupied and it would be for her to say what she was going to do next. But how could she before he had asked her definitely to marry him? And would they marry soon, or was she to go back to the hospital for a while? When he didn't speak she said cheerfully: 'Oh, I'll take care—I'm going

to have a lazy morning anyway, because your
mother is going to visit a friend in Hoenderloo.'

'Oh, Jonkvrouwe de Tielle, they're great cronies.'
He picked up his letters and stuffed them into his
jacket pocket, came round the table to kiss her, said
easily: 'I'll see you this evening then, Britannia,'
and went away, leaving her determined to ask him
what was the matter and what was more, to get an
answer.

She frowned as she poured herself more coffee.
He could have told her that he was visiting Madeleine that afternoon, he could have told her even
why he wanted to see her in the first place. Surely
two people who were going to marry didn't have
secrets from each other—not that kind of secret,
anyway. But perhaps, because she hadn't been quite
definite about marrying him, he didn't feel bound to
tell her such things. She told herself that she was
being a little unreasonable and admitted that she was
jealous.

And later that day, as she was getting ready for
dinner in her room, she could see that it was she
who had been at fault; Jake had come home, rather
late it was true, but his usual charming self, and
although his kiss had been a casual one, he had
joined in the talk and when she had peeped at him,
the frown had gone; he looked relieved…so it had
been something to do with Madeleine, and whatever

it was had been settled. Britannia, viewing herself in the green dress in the cheval mirror between the windows, decided that she didn't look at all bad; it was wonderful what relief did to one's face. She went carefully downstairs, with due regard to the ankle, and spent a pleasant evening. Mevrouw Luitingh van Thien had brought her friend back with her and after dinner the four of them played bridge—not a very serious rubber, which was a good thing, because Britannia was a more than indifferent player.

When she got down to breakfast the next morning it was to find Jake already gone. 'The professor was called out in the night, miss,' Marinus informed her, 'a nasty accident on the motorway. He came home to change and shower and eat his breakfast and was gone again by half past seven. A busy day ahead of him, I understand, miss.'

She agreed and thanked him, adding: 'Marinus, you speak such very good English—have you lived in England?'

He coughed in a gratified way. 'My family lived in Arnhem, miss. I had a good deal to do with the British soldiers at one time.'

'Underground?' asked Britannia, very interested.

'You might say so, miss. Everyone in these parts was more or less involved. I came here as a young man and the professor's father saw to it that I had

English lessons; he found it a waste that I should have picked up so much of the language, and not always as correct as it should be.'

'Oh, Marinus, how nice—and isn't it fortunate for me and anyone else here who can't speak Dutch?'

'It has had its uses, miss. Can I fetch you some fresh coffee?'

'No, thanks. The professor suggested that I went to the library and had a good look at the books. I think I'll do that. Mevrouw Luitingh van Thien will be out, won't she?'

'Yes, miss. I will serve your coffee in the library presently, and I think that lunch in the little sitting room might be more comfortable for you.'

Britannia got up and went to the door. She wasn't using her stick any more now; her ankle was just about cured. 'Thank you, Marinus, that does sound nice.' She smiled at him as she went out and he beamed back. She was a nice young lady, he thought, and would make a good mistress to work for.

Britannia spent a pleasant morning; she had never seen so many books outside a public library before, not only rare first editions but a comprehensive collection of all the most readable books, and a reference section which had her absorbed until Marinus, coming quiet-footed to remove the coffee tray, told her that her lunch was about to be set on the table.

She had intended to go back to the library after the meal, but the sitting room was cosy and an armchair and a book by the fire was very appealing; she fetched an old crimson-bound volume of *Punch* and settled down happily for the afternoon. The house was quiet and already the winter dusk was creeping into the room. She switched on a reading lamp and opened the book. Perhaps Jake would be home in time for tea; he had had a long day, if he wasn't too tired she would ask him about the future. She hadn't done it yesterday; somehow there hadn't been the chance.

The door bell rang almost before she had turned the first page and she looked up, wondering who it could be; Mevrouw Luitingh van Thien was still out and didn't intend to return until the early evening. If it was a visitor it would be awkward, for her few words of Dutch would prove quite inadequate when it came to conversation. Perhaps whoever it was would speak English or even go away.

She turned to look over her shoulder as the door opened and Marinus came in, but before he could speak Madeleine had swept past him and shut the door in his face.

Britannia felt a quiver of rage which changed to amazement; this wasn't the Madeleine she knew, despite the tempestuous entry; this was a subdued, rather untidy girl who hadn't bothered much with her face or hair either. She stared at her, quite star-tled, hardly recognising her, and got out of her chair. 'You're ill!' she exclaimed.

Madeleine shook her head. 'No, I'm all right. I've been worried—I am worried now, for I have been trying to make up my mind to come and talk to you, but I think that you may not believe me, and why should you?' She shrugged her shoulders in a re-signed way. 'Even now I do not think that it will be of any use, but I must try...'

'It's about Jake.' Britannia felt cold as she said it.

Madeleine nodded. 'Yes—you see, I wish to be honest with you—it's about Jake.'

'And this—whatever it is you want to tell me—is it important to you, or to him? And I'm not sure I want to hear it. And why can't you wait until he is here and tell him too?'

'He already knows.'

They were facing each other across the charming room. 'You want to make trouble,' declared Britan-nia, not mincing matters.

Madeleine came a step nearer. 'I don't like you, Britannia, why should I? But it is necessary that we talk; I do not wish to make trouble, but if I do not speak now, then there may be much unhappiness later on.'

Britannia was puzzled; Madeleine sounded sin-cere and she looked white and strained. Perhaps she had misjudged her after all. 'I'm listening,' she said steadily.

Madeleine didn't sit down. 'You must know that I expected to marry Jake, and I own that it was a shock when I heard that it was you whom he had chosen... You see, we have known each other for years.' She looked away for a moment. 'But there's more to it than that; are you quite sure that he wants to marry you? I mean, does he love you—a lasting love one needs for marriage?'

She looked briefly at Britannia, her face solemn. 'You are pretty and you amuse him because you speak your mind to him and he finds that diverting, but perhaps in a little while he will not be diverted any more, only irritated. You see, there is a gulf between you, Britannia. You do not come from his circle of friends. He met you in an unusual manner, did he not, so you are—how do you say?—attractive to him, but if that wears thin, what is there left? You do not know how to run a large house such as this one, nor how to entertain guests as he would want them entertained; you do not dress very well, you do not even speak his language. Even if he thinks that he loves you now, will there not come a day when these things will prove a barrier between you? Can you honestly tell me that this will not happen?'

Britannia got up and walked over to a window and looked out. The grey day outside reflected her feelings. 'I don't think that one can be certain of anything,' she said, and forced her voice to sound reasonable. Madeleine had touched unerringly on her own doubts, but she wasn't going to let her see that. And she hadn't said anything she hadn't herself already thought of.

Madeleine went on: 'I expect you thought that it was I who wanted to marry Jake, and that he has never loved me, but I can prove that he does—that his love for you isn't love at all, only infatuation, that he is already regretting...'

Britannia didn't look round, so that she didn't see Madeleine's quick glance, calculating and sly as she opened her bag and took out an envelope and crossed the room to give it to her. It was addressed to Madeleine in the professor's writing and it had been opened, and the letter she pulled out was in his writing too; Britannia would have recognised that atrocious scrawl anywhere.

'It's in Dutch,' said Madeleine, 'but I'll translate it and it will explain everything to you.' She held out the letter to Britannia with a sudden gesture which Britannia quite misinterpreted, and she saw the first words: '*Mijn lieveling...*' She couldn't see any more, because of the way the letter was folded, but she knew that it meant 'my darling', just as she knew that unlike the English word, the Dutch used it only as a term of real endearment between two people. And as though Madeleine had read her thoughts, she said quietly: 'You must know that we don't use the word *lieveling* in the social sense as the English do—it means much more to us than that.' She unfolded the letter and came a little nearer to show Jake's name at the end of the page, and Britannia, looking at it, thought dully that there must be a mistake. She drew a breath and said: 'I don't think I want to hear it, thank you.'

'But you must,' insisted Madeleine, 'otherwise you will never believe me. Why should you when you know that Jake and I...' She shot another look at Britannia, who had gone back to her chair, sitting there with her hands folded so quietly in her lap. 'I owe it to us all to be honest, and I am trying to be that.' She sounded very sincere.

She opened the letter and went to the window to read it. 'It begins: "My darling..."'

'No,' said Britannia sharply, but Madeleine took no notice. '"We see so little of each other and there is so much that I want to tell you—to explain how I could have imagined myself in love—but only a little—with someone else when you were there, waiting for me, for you knew it sooner than I. I intend to see her and tell her that it is you I will marry, and I think that she will understand, for her feeling for me cannot be deep. Perhaps you are wondering why I have not told you this instead of writing it, but somehow the time and place have never been right.'' It ends: ''All my love, Jake.'''

'When did you get this letter?' asked Britannia in a dry little voice.

'Marinus brought it round this morning.' Madeleine walked deliberately to the bell rope by the fireplace. 'I'll ring for Marinus to come here—you will believe him.' Her voice was so bitter that Britannia said at once:

'There's no need for that. I've seen the letter, haven't I?' She stirred in her chair. 'Jake went to see you yesterday, didn't he?'

'Yes, and I had to see you first...'

Britannia glanced at the clock. Jake would be home soon and she wondered what he was going to say. Madeleine said quietly: 'Men like new faces even though they still love the old.' She was putting on her coat, ready to go, and Britannia got to her feet and said in a polite voice:

'Thank you for coming. I'm—I'm sure you have done what you think is right and at least I know what to do...' She drew a breath to steady her voice. 'I'm sure you'll be very happy together,' and then: 'I didn't know that you loved each other.'

Madeleine didn't answer her as she went.

The professor came into his house half an hour later, during which time Britannia had tried to sort out her thoughts and had failed lamentably. There was so much truth in what Madeleine had told her and she had sounded sincere; moreover, she had looked upset, not sure of herself, and the letter had been genuine…

So it was that when Jake entered the room she voiced her thoughts without allowing common sense to control them. 'You went to see Madeleine yesterday.'

He paused on his way across the room and gave her a long look. 'I did.' The smile on his lips had gone and his mouth had taken on a rather grim look. Britannia saw it and plunged still further.

'She told me you had—and it was in the letter, and although I believed her I thought there might be a mistake—that I hadn't understood…'

'Nor have I understood, Britannia. I take it that Madeleine has been here?' He frowned. 'And you speak of a letter?' His eyes had narrowed and Britannia said quickly before she lost her courage:

'The letter you wrote to her, of course. She showed it to me—well, the beginning and end with your name. I didn't want to see any more of it, I didn't want to hear it either, but she insisted on translating it, otherwise she said I wouldn't have believed her.'

'But you did believe her, my dear Britannia,' he observed blandly, 'without giving me the benefit of the doubt, too.' There was a nasty curl to his lip.

'Oh, dear,' cried Britannia in an exasperated voice, 'now you're in a fine temper…'

'Not yet, but I believe I shall be very shortly,' he agreed silkily. 'I thought that you trusted me, Britannia.'

She looked at him helplessly, aware that she had started all wrong and it was going to be difficult to put it right—indeed, she had the strongest suspicion that he wasn't going to listen to anything she said. 'Shall we talk about it later?' she asked quietly. 'It was my fault, jumping on you like that.'

'We will talk about it now.' He had become all at once arrogant as well as angry, and it was all so much worse because he was so coldly polite. 'If I am to be accused of—what shall we call it? Double dealing? Philandering? then I would prefer to settle the matter now and not, as you had no doubt hoped, after I had been softened with a whisky and a good dinner.'

Britannia stamped her good foot, careless of what she said now. 'You're impossible!' she told him bitterly. 'You won't listen—you don't want to. There must be some explanation, only you won't give it, only snarl at me. And you are bad-tempered and arrogant and now you won't listen…'

'Not listen?' his voice was all silk again. 'My dear girl, what else am I doing but listening, most unwillingly, to your tirade?'

'Oh, it's not—it's not, and I expected you to tell me,' she went on desperately.

He lifted his brows. 'I have no intention of telling you anything.' He smiled mockingly. 'Madeleine seems to have done that for me.' He added: 'And you believed her.'

Britannia regarded him with hopeless eyes. 'It's Madeleine you love and want to marry—she said so. I wouldn't have believed it, only there was the letter.'

'Ah, yes, this letter. And you imagined that I would—what is the old-fashioned term—trifle with your affections and then drop you when it suited me?'

'That's only one way of looking at it,' she pointed out fiercely.

'The only way, Britannia.' He wandered over to the fireplace and kicked a log into flames. 'And if that is how you feel about it, there is nothing more to be said.'

Britannia's insides went cold. 'Jake, please don't let's quarrel...'

He turned to look at her over his shoulder. 'I never quarrel, I say what I have to say and that is all.'

'It's not, you know,' cried Britannia in a high voice. 'You haven't said anything, only made nasty remarks.' Her voice quavered for a moment, 'I thought we were honest with each other…'

His face was bland and expressionless. 'What would be the point of being honest with you, my dear girl? You have condemned me unheard and that, in my judgment at least, makes honesty between us quite pointless.' He added, 'I'm not sure what I should have explained to you, but nothing, and I mean nothing, would force me to do so now, even if I knew what it was.'

'But Jake, you do know.'

'Perhaps I can guess.' His smile mocked her again. 'But anything I had intended to tell you when I came into this room is quite purposeless now.'

CHAPTER NINE

'I THINK I should go home,' said Britannia slowly.

'Of course you will go home.' The professor was in a towering rage, his eyes like blue ice, the nostrils of his magnificent nose flaring with his temper. 'I shall drive you there myself.' He glanced at his watch. 'We should be able to catch the night ferry from the Hoek. I imagine that half an hour is time enough in which to pack.'

Britannia goggled at him. 'Half an hour? The night ferry? Jake, you're in a most shocking rage and you don't know what you're saying.'

'Indeed I am in a rage, but I am quite aware of what I am saying. We should arrive at your home during tomorrow afternoon.'

'You're not coming with me.' She spoke defiantly.

'Yes, I am.' He glared quite ferociously at her. 'You wish to leave my house as soon as possible; the least I can do is to speed you on your way and make sure that you arrive home.'

She swallowed the great lump in her throat. 'Jake, please—you must try and understand. I can't hurt

Madeleine—I hate her, you know that, and that's all the more reason…'

'I understand very well. I also understand that you have no compunction in hurting me.' His sneering voice made her shudder.

She was almost in tears now, but it would never do to cry. She said in a calm little voice which shook just a little, 'Jake, could we talk about it? You haven't given me a chance…and you haven't told me…'

His cold voice cut through her muddle. 'Why should I tell you anything? You already know.'

It was hopeless; he was angry because she had discovered that he really loved Madeleine before he had found a way to tell her himself. 'You'll forget me,' she told him miserably.

His smile was nasty. 'I have no intention of discussing the matter with you, Britannia. Like all women you have rushed into a situation without stopping to think.'

'I have thought!' snapped Britannia, stung by the memory of the last few hours. 'I've thought so much that I don't know my own mind any more.'

'So I perceive.' His voice was all silk. 'And now if you care to go and pack and say goodbye to my mother…?'

He held the door open and there was nothing else for her to do but to go through it.

A little over half an hour later, sitting beside the professor as he sent the Rolls racing down the motorway which would take them to the Hoek, Britannia reflected that it was like being in a nightmare where one wishes desperately to do something and is prevented by other people and circumstances. She had packed in a daze and then gone to wish Mevrouw Luitingh van Thien goodbye, and because there had been no time to explain, she had stated baldly that she wasn't going to marry Jake after all and that he was taking her home there and then.

His mother had said very little. 'A misunderstanding,' she had observed severely, 'and of course Jake is in one of his rages and won't allow anyone to say a word. I'm sorry, my dear—you were, still are, the right wife for him.'

Britannia let that pass even though she agreed with every word. 'He insists upon taking me all the way to Moreton,' she said helplessly.

'And quite right too. I hope you will have a good journey, Britannia.' She had offered a cheek and then added: 'It is Madeleine, of course.'

'Yes,' said Britannia, 'it is. Jake will forget me.'

'A pity that there is no time to tell me the whole. Jake has, of course, said nothing.'

Britannia had walked to the door and with her hand on the handle, had said miserably: 'He loves her,' and then gone out to where Jake waited for her.

The professor might be in a rage, but he had it under control now; his flow of light conversation would have done credit to a seasoned diplomat making the best of a bad situation. Throughout the journey he was never at a loss for a topic; not that Britannia had much idea of what he was saying. Once she tried to stop him, but her desperate: 'Jake, please could we…?' was ignored as he went into a detailed account of the rulers of Holland. Britannia, bogged down in a succession of Willems and the Spanish Occupation, said 'Oh, really?' and 'Indeed,' every now and then while she tried to sort out her thoughts. But they were still only as far as Koningin Emma when they reached the Hoek and began the business of getting on board. Presumably the professor had found the time to telephone for tickets, for there was no delay in getting the car on board and after a polite goodnight, Britannia was led away to a comfortable cabin and presently a stewardess appeared with a tray of coffee and sandwiches, and the information that tea and toast would be brought in the morning.

Britannia drank all the coffee and nibbled at a sandwich and then, because there seemed nothing else to do, undressed and got into the narrow little bed. It was going to be a rough crossing judging by the way the boat was lurching out into the North Sea; not that that mattered. As far as she was concerned, it could sink with all hands and her with it for all she cared. But although she lay awake, she was quite unable to think sensibly. The arrival of her morning tea was a relief and she drank it thankfully, got up and dressed, made up her white face very carefully and then, uncertain as to what to do next, sat down on the stool by the bed and waited in a kind of daze, not thinking at all for by now she was too tired.

When a voice over the intercom told everyone to rejoin their car she picked up her bag and opened the door. The professor was outside, leaning against the wall. He gave her an icily courteous good morning, told her to follow him, took her bag and strode off. In the car presently, waiting to disembark, there was too much noise to talk, and presently going through the routine of landing there was no need to say more than a word or two, but once on the road to London the professor broke his silence.

'Rather a rough crossing,' he remarked pleasantly. 'I hope you weren't too disturbed?'

All she could think of to say was: 'Not at all, thank you,' but the baldness of this reply didn't deter him from keeping up a steady flow of small talk. It lasted right through Colchester and down the A12 and around the northern perimeter of London until they eventually joined the M3 at the Chertsey round-about. Jake turned off again almost at once, remarking that she would probably like a cup of coffee, and drove the few miles to Chobham where he drew up before the Four Seasons restaurant and invited her to get out. Britannia shivered as she did so, for it was a chilly morning and she was tired and empty, but the coffee put new heart into her and she got into the car feeling more able to cope with the situation, until it struck her forcibly that very shortly she would be home now and her parents would expect some explanation. It was only too likely that they would dash forward with cries of welcome for their supposedly future son-in-law. Just as though he had read her mind, Jake said silkily: 'Have you got your speech ready? Do say anything you wish—don't mind me.' He added: 'I have broad shoulders.'

She blinked back tears, stupidly wanting to weep her eyes red because he had broad shoulders and large, clever hands and a handsome face, and very soon now she wouldn't see them again. She mumbled: 'I don't know what I'm going to say,' and cried pettishly: 'Oh, can't you see? I'm not doing or saying any of the things I want to…words are being put in my mouth. I'm forced to come home, there's so much I want to say and you haven't the patience to listen—what am I to do?'

'My dear girl, surely I am the last person to ask?'

She kept quiet after that while the Rolls swallowed the miles in its well-bred way until he turned off at Ringwood, went through the little town and travelled on to Ibsley where they lunched at The Old Beams. It was a well-known restaurant and the food was delicious, but Britannia ate what was put before her without noticing what it was, making a great effort to match her companion's relaxed manner and failing, did she but know it, miserably. They didn't linger over the meal, but drove on, back on to the A31, through Wimborne Minster and Bere Regis, to turn off on to a side road and then turn off again to Moreton. An early dusk was falling by now, and as they approached the cottage, Britannia could see that there were lights already shining cosily from its windows. 'It's here,' she said, and bade an unspoken goodbye to the Rolls as he opened her door and she got out.

Her mother answered the door and after a surprised moment cried: 'Darling—how lovely, and you've brought Jake with you...' She stopped there because she had seen Britannia's face, white and rigid, certainly not the look of a happy girl. 'Come in, both of you,' she continued, 'you must be cold.' She peered over the professor's broad shoulders and saw the Rolls. 'Well, probably not, in that car, but I'm sure you could do with a cup of tea.'

She submitted to Britannia's hug and held out her

hand to Jake. 'I'm so glad to meet you,' she told him. 'Come and meet my husband.'

They were all in the sitting room, with Britannia taking off her coat while the two men shook hands and her father, rightly interpreting her mother's look, forbore from making any of the remarks fathers usually make on such occasions. Instead he asked about their journey, remarked upon the weather, begged his visitor to remove his coat and then embraced his daughter with a cheerful: 'How nice to have you home, Britannia—for Christmas, I hope?'

He didn't wait for her answer; even his loving but not very discerning eye could see that she was holding back tears, so he invited the professor to sit down and engaged him in conversation while tea was brought in and sandwiches eaten, and the professor, at his most charming, didn't look at Britannia at all but said presently: 'This has been delightful, but I must start back. I intend to catch the night boat.'

Britannia looked at the clock on the mantelpiece. 'It's almost five o'clock, you'll never do it in the time.'

He smiled at her quite nicely. 'What a pity that we can't bet on that,' he told her. 'As it is, I'm afraid you'll have to guess whether I do or not.'

He made his farewells quickly, including Britannia in them without actually speaking to her, and to her thanks for bringing her home he murmured: 'As I have already told you, Britannia, it was the least I could do.'

He didn't wish her goodbye, only smiled a little thinly at her. Her mother and father saw him to the door, but she stayed where she was, not moving until she heard the last murmur of the Rolls' engine die away.

Mr and Mrs Smith came back into the room together and Britannia said at once in a high voice: 'You must be wondering…I told you that I'd found the man I wanted to marry, didn't I, and it seemed as though I would; everything went right for me— well, most of the time. I—I thought he loved me even though there was this other girl.' She looked at her mother. '*Vogue* and *Harpers* and utterly beautiful—you know what I mean.' She lapsed into silence and her parents waited patiently, not saying a word. 'She was furious, of course, and she hated me—still does. We didn't see much of each other, and then the day before yesterday she came to Jake's house and showed me a letter from him; not all of it, but enough to make me see…'

'In Dutch or English?' asked her father quietly.

'Oh, Dutch, because it was to her, of course, but she translated it for me…'

'You are sure it was to her?'

Britannia nodded, 'It began "*Lieveling*", that's darling, and it was his writing and his name at the bottom, and the envelope was addressed to her. She offered to show me the whole letter, but she was so quiet and sad and she couldn't have invented all of it. She told me she hated me, but she thought that if I married Jake and he still loved her, I would be miserable if I found out, and he would be wretched as soon as he had recovered from his infatuation, tied to me and loving her...'

'He brought you home,' observed her mother softly.

'He's the kind of man who does his duty,' said Britannia bitterly.

Her mother asked: 'And did Jake mind very much when you told him you weren't going to marry him?'

'He wouldn't even discuss it, he—he was furiously angry; he has a very nasty temper.'

Her mother nodded. 'But I don't quite see why he should have been so angry. After all, if he loved this girl all the time and was only passing the time of day with you, he should have been glad that you had found out about it—it saved him having to tell you, didn't it?'

Britannia sniffed. 'He likes to do things his way— I expect he'd got it all planned how he wanted it. It's over now, anyway.' She began to collect the tea things on to the tray. 'May I use the telephone? I thought I'd ring the hospital and start straight away—I've ten days to work still, then if I may I'll come home for Christmas and find another job.'

'Of course, dear. Your father will help me with the washing up; you telephone now and get it fixed up.' Her mother picked up the tray. 'Your ankle will stand up to it?'

'Well, I think so, I thought I'd ask if I could work somewhere where there's not such a rush.'

'Geriatrics,' she was told by the Senior Nursing Officer. The ward Sister there had gone off sick and Britannia's return was providential, and could she report for duty as soon as possible?

A day or two at home would have been nice; on the other hand, if she went back on the next day and saved her days off, she would be finished before Christmas; she agreed to report for duty the following afternoon, and went to tell her mother, and that astute woman said not another word about Jake but for the rest of the evening discussed plans for Christmas and sent Britannia early to bed. 'Father will drive you up,' she said comfortably. 'You can leave after breakfast and that will give you plenty of time.'

So Britannia retired to her room and unpacked and repacked a smaller case and went to bed, to lie awake and think of Jake and then force her thoughts to the future.

The geriatric wards of St Jude's weren't in the main hospital but five minutes' walk away, down a narrow street made gloomy by the blank walls of warehouses. There wasn't a tree in sight nor yet a blade of grass, and the annexe itself was an old workhouse, red brick and elaborate at that on the outside and a labyrinth of narrow passages, stone staircases and long wards into which the sun never seemed to shine. And yet the best had been made of a bad job; the walls were distempered in pastel colours, the counterpanes were gay patchwork, there were flowers here and there and sensible easy chairs grouped together round little tables so that those who were able could sit and gossip. To most of them, the place had been home for many months and probably would be for the rest of their lives, and Britannia, eyeing the female wards which were to be her especial care, supposed that it was probably a better home than the solitary bedsitter so many of them occupied. True, they hadn't their independence any more, and most of them set great store by that, but they had regular food, warmth, company and a little money each week which they could spend when the shop lady came round with her trolley, and some of them, though regrettably few, had families who came to see them.

Britannia took the report from the agency nurse who had been called in to plug the gap and settled down at her desk to read the patients' notes before she did a round. She had been a little surprised when she arrived at the hospital at lunch time to be asked if she would go on duty immediately, but she hadn't minded. Having something to do would get through the days and if she had enough work she would be tired enough to sleep. She had been given her old room in the nurses' home; she didn't bother to unpack but got straight into uniform, donned her cloak against the cold, and hurried along the miserable little street to the annexe. Sitting at the desk, it seemed to her that she had never been away from the hospital and yet so much had been crowded into those few weeks, and the whole telescoped into the quick journey home again. She thanked heaven silently for understanding parents; a pity she wouldn't be going home for her days off, but if she saved them up she would be able to leave two days sooner. Eight days, she told herself with false cheerfulness, and buried her pretty head in the pile of notes before her.

She went to see Joan when she got off duty that evening; a very excited Joan, her head full of plans for her wedding, but she paused presently to ask: 'Why Geriatrics, ducky? Isn't the ankle up to the rush and scurry of Men's Surgical? And I had a letter from Mevrouw Veske saying that you would have some wonderful news for me.' She paused to look at Britannia's face. 'But I can see that she's wrong. Do you want to talk about it?'

'No, not now, Joan. I'm only on Geriatrics for a week, then I'm leaving.'

'You're not getting…no, of course not. It's that professor, isn't it?'

'Yes. Now tell me more about your wedding…'

The geriatric wards might have been easy on her ankle, but their occupants made heavy demands on Britannia. They had taken to her at once and most of them saw in her a kind of daughter, there to fulfil their many and several wants; she was also Staff, someone who gave them their pills, saw that they had their treatments and got up in the morning and went to bed in the evening, ate their meals, and twice a day did a round of the wards, stopping to talk to each of them. The nursing was undemanding but heavy and Britannia had a staff of part-time nurses and auxiliaries, but still it was tiring and she was thankful for that; it meant that she slept for a good deal of the night. All the same, the first two days dragged even though she filled her off-duty with Christmas shopping, willing herself not to think of Jake at all. It didn't work, of course. She thought of him all the time, he was there beside her, behind every door she opened, round every corner, beneath her eyelids when she closed them at night.

On the third morning she went on duty with a

headache and the nasty empty feeling induced by too little sleep and too many meals missed, and when she had taken the night nurse's report the Senior Nursing Officer telephoned to say that the part-time staff nurse who was to do the evening duty wouldn't be able to come in, and would Britannia mind very much filling in for her. 'You can save it up and leave half a day sooner,' said the voice cheerfully, 'and you should manage an hour's quiet this afternoon during visiting.'

Britannia thought that very unlikely; visitors liked to talk to Sister, the patients who hadn't anyone to see them tended to make little demands of her because they felt lonely and left out...she said she didn't mind and heard the Senior Nursing Officer's relieved sigh as she put down the receiver.

She realised as soon as she went into the first ward that the day had begun badly; for one thing, it was a grey, cold morning, and despite the gay counterpanes and bright walls, the grey had filtered in, making the patients morose and unwilling to stir from their nice warm beds. Britannia set about the patient task of cheering them up, an exercise which took a great deal of the morning. Luckily it was the consultant's weekly round, one of the highlights in the old ladies' week, and they had brightened up considerably by the time Doctor Payne and his houseman arrived. He was a good doctor, nearing retirement; Britannia had had her medical lectures from him when she was in training and he had always been pleasant to the nurses, even when those on night duty had fallen asleep under his very nose, or the brighter ones had asked obvious questions in order to show off. He remembered her at once and observed forthrightly: 'Staff Nurse Smith—I thought you were a surgical girl. Been ill? You look under the weather.'

'I'm fine, Doctor Payne, a bit tired, that's all. I'm filling in a few days before I leave.'

'Getting married?' he wanted to know. 'All the pretty girls get married just as they're getting useful. Who's the lucky man?'

'There isn't one. I—I just wanted a change of scene.'

Doctor Payne shot her a look, said 'Um,' and then: 'Well, well,' and coughed. 'And how are my old ladies?'

She gave him a brief report and they started off. The round took some time, for although most of the patients had nothing dramatic wrong with them they had a variety of tiresome complaints and aches and pains, all of which had to be discussed and if necessary treated. It was time to serve dinners when Doctor Payne had at last finished and after that there were the old ladies to settle for their afternoon rest and then the medicines to give out. Britannia went to her own dinner rather late and ate tepid beef and potatoes and carrots and remembered all the delicious food she had eaten in Jake's house, so that she rejected the milk pudding offered her and went with the other staff nurses at her table to drink the cup of tea they always managed to squeeze into their dinner break, however short. The talk was all of Christmas, so that she was able to parry the few questions she was asked about her trip to Holland and trail the red herring of Joan's approaching wedding across her listeners' path. They broke up presently to go back on duty and Britannia made her solitary way back to the annexe.

Her superior's hopeful suggestion that she should take an hour off during visiting hour came to nothing, of course; there were fewer visitors than usual, which meant that the old ladies made a continuous demand on her and the nurses on duty. It didn't seem worth going back to the hospital for tea; she had a tray in her office before getting on with the evening's work, and when it was time to go to supper, she decided not to go to that either; she wasn't hungry and she could make herself some toast later. The wards were quiet now, with all the patients back in bed, most of them already dozing lightly. Britannia sent her two nurses to supper, finished her report and then went softly round the wards, saying a quiet goodnight to each old lady. It was at the bottom of the second ward, when she was almost through, that she found Mrs Thorn out of bed.

'Now don't you be vexed,' said Mrs Thorn in a cheerful whisper. 'I just took a fancy to sit out for a bit longer and I got that nice little nurse to put me back in the chair for half an hour, and don't go blaming her, because I told her you'd said that I could.' She laughed gently. 'I'll go back now you're here.'

Britannia hid a smile. Mrs Thorn was the oldest inhabitant in the Geriatric Unit and was consequently a little spoilt. She said without meaning it: 'You're a naughty old thing, aren't you? But doing something different is fun sometimes, isn't it?'

Mrs Thorn was small and fragile and very old, with birdlike bones knotted and twisted by arthritis. Britannia lifted her out of the chair and popped her gently into her bed. It took a little time to get the old lady's dressing gown off, for Mrs Thorn liked things done just so and she enjoyed a chat too. Britannia was tucking in the patchwork quilt when she became aware that someone was walking down the ward, to stop at the foot of the bed. Jake, elegant and calm and self-assured as always. Mrs Thorn, with the childlike outspokenness of the old, broke a silence which for Britannia seemed to go on for ever and ever.

'And who are you?' she demanded in a piping

voice. 'A handsome, well-set-up man like you shouldn't be here. You should be out with some pretty girl, or better still by your own fireside with a wife and children to share it.' She smiled suddenly and caught at Britannia's hand. 'Perhaps you've come to fetch our dear Staff Nurse away? She's a lovely young thing and she shouldn't be here— we're all so old...'

The professor was looking at her gravely, without even glancing at Britannia.

'I hope that when Britannia here is your age, my dear, she will be as charming as you, and yes, I have come to fetch her; she's my girl, you see, and although I haven't a wife and children I hope she will soon fill that gap for me.'

He spoke loudly so that several of the old ladies in nearby beds popped up from beneath their blankets, nodding and smiling their approval.

'Oh, hush,' begged Britannia, quite forgetting unhappiness and misery and tiredness in the delight of seeing him again. 'Everyone is listening.'

He looked at her then, his eyes very blue and bright. 'And I am glad of it, my darling. The more who hear me say that I love you, the better. Perhaps if I repeat it a sufficient number of times and in a loud enough voice before as many people as possible, you will bring yourself to believe that I mean it.'

Britannia still held Mrs Thorn's bony little claw in her own capable hand. 'Oh, Jake...but you must explain—Madeleine told me...'

The professor sat himself down on the end of Mrs Thorn's bed and stretched his long legs before him as though he intended to stay a long time. 'Ah, yes,' his voice was still much too loud and clear. 'Well, dearest girl, if you will hold that delightful tongue of yours for ten minutes I will endeavour to do that.'

'Not here, you don't,' declared Britannia, aware that old eyes and ears were tuned in all round them, 'and not now. I'm on duty until eight o'clock and then I should go to supper—I haven't been yet.'

She trembled as she said it in case he walked away in a temper because he wasn't getting his own way, but she wasn't going to give way easily. There was still Madeleine's shadow between them; she would have to be explained.

The professor spoke with such extreme mildness that she cast him a suspicious look which he met with such tenderness that she had to look quickly away again in case she weakened.

'I've had no supper myself, perhaps we might have it together.'

Britannia tucked Mrs Thorn in carefully. 'Have you been here long?' she asked. A silly question really, but she had to say something ordinary; her head might be in the clouds, but she had to keep her feet on the ground.

'I landed at Dover three hours ago.'

She retied the ribbon at the end of Mrs Thorn's wispy pigtail.

'Oh?...'

'I knew you were here,' he supplied smoothly, 'because I telephoned your mother and asked before I left home.' He got up off the bed. 'How long will you be, Britannia?'

'Another ten minutes. But I have to go back to the Home and change...'

'I'll be outside.' He wished Mrs Thorn and the other eagerly listening ladies a good night and went away. Britannia, watching him go, wondered as she saw the ward doors swing gently after him, if she had had a dream, an idea Mrs Thorn quickly scotched.

'Now that's what I call an 'andsome man, Staff Nurse. He'll make you a fine husband.'

Oh, he would, agreed Britannia silently, but only if he made it very clear about Madeleine. She forced her mind to good sense, wished Mrs Thorn a good night, visited the remaining patients, answering a spate of excited questions as she did so, and went to give the report to the night nurses.

They were already in the office and the night staff nurse hardly waited for her to reach for the Kardex before she exclaimed: 'I say, Britannia, there's a Rolls at the door and the most super man in it.' She stared hard at Britannia as she said it; she had heard rumours in the hospital. 'Is he the boy-friend?'

Britannia said deliberately: 'Mrs Tweedy, bed one... He's the man I'm going to marry.' She hadn't really meant to say that, but as she did she knew without a doubt that was just what she intended doing, even if she never got to the bottom of the riddle of Madeleine. Before anyone could say a word, she went on: 'A good day, Mist.Mag.Tri. given TDS. She's to have physiotherapy by order of Doctor Payne. Mrs Scott, bed two...'

The report didn't take very long. She handed over the keys, wished the nurses goodnight and went down to the entrance, her cloak over her arm, the bits and pieces she had found necessary to have with her during the day in a tote bag. She had quite forgotten to do anything to her face or her hair, but it didn't matter. She was so happy that a shiny nose and hair all anyhow went unnoticed.

The professor was in the hall, a bleak dark brown place no one had had sufficient money to modernise. It had a centre light, a grim white glass globe which did nothing for the complexions for those beneath its cold rays. Britannia didn't notice it; she came to a halt before Jake and said a little shyly, 'I have to go to the main hospital and change.'

He took her bag from her and fastened the cloak carefully. 'No, there's no need. We'll go to Ned's Café, where we first met. I suspect, dear heart, that I have a romantic nature.'

'It'll be full…'

'No matter, the more people there the better. If necessary I shall go down on my knees.'

Britannia choked on a laugh. 'You can't—you simply can't…'

'I simply can.' He swooped suddenly and kissed her. 'That's better—let's go.'

The Rolls looked a little out of place parked outside Ned's place, and one or two people turned to stare at them as they went inside. There was an empty table in the middle of the room and the professor led the way to it, wishing those around him a courteous good evening as he went, and when Ned came over with a pleased: 'Well, I never, Staff— I'aven't seen you for weeks, nor you neither, sir. What's it to be?' He ordered bacon sandwiches and toasted cheese and a pot of tea, and when Ned had gone again: 'You're pale, my darling, and there are shadows under your eyes…'

'Well, of course there are! I've been… Jake, you must explain.'

'Of course. Here is our tea.'

Ned lingered for a few minutes and Britannia's hand shook a little with impatience as she poured the strong brew. But Jake didn't seem impatient at all; indeed, he entered into quite a conversation about the hospital rugger team so that when Ned at last took himself off, Britannia said quite fiercely: 'I want to know…and all you can do is talk about rugger!'

'My darling, I was a rugger player myself—besides, I have a soft spot for Ned. He is, as it were, our fairy godfather.'

The bacon sandwiches arrived then and a moment later the cheese and then Ned went away to serve a party of six who had just come in. The professor passed the sandwiches and only after Britannia had eaten almost a whole one did he say: 'Before I say anything, I want you to read this.' He took a folded letter from his pocket and handed it across the table to her.

She saw what it was immediately. 'But why should I? I mean, it was written to Madeleine.'

He gave her a quizzical look. 'Was it? My dear Britannia, all at sea, aren't you? Read it.'

She read it silently, pausing once to look at him. He was sitting back watching her with a tender smile. She finished it and then read it for a second time, more slowly.

'It was for me,' she whispered. 'She found it…Marinus didn't take it.'

'Yes, love.'

'But the envelope—she showed it to me...'

'And if you had looked carefully you would have seen that it was in Madeleine's own hand. You see, my darling, you expected to see my writing on the envelope, didn't you, and so you did.'

She folded the letter carefully and held it in her hand. 'What a fool,' she said, 'but you could have told me,' she began, and then: 'No, of course you wouldn't have done that—you thought that I didn't believe you.'

'I see that you have a tremendous insight into my failings, dearest, so useful in a wife.'

She poured more strong tea for them both and the professor asked quietly: 'Will you marry me, Britannia?'

She put her cup down. 'Oh, Jake, yes—you know I will!'

'I have a special licence with me, we can marry tomorrow at your home.'

For a moment Britannia had no words. The thought that there could be nothing nicer than to get up from the rickety little table and just go home without more ado and marry Jake in the morning lingered for a few seconds in her head before she said: 'But I can't, Jake. I've another four days—I should have to pack and...'

'You can if you want to. I've dealt with all that. I don't know how important the packing is—half an hour? Your mother said she would leave the door for us and something on the stove.'

'Mother? How does she know?'

'I telephoned yesterday to say that we would be coming. Your father was kind enough to advise me about the licence.'

'I thought it took days...'

'A day or so, yes. I telephoned him when I got back to Holland and found out about Madeleine.'

Britannia bit into a sandwich. 'How did you do that?' she wanted to know.

'I asked her what she had done. Will you mind very much if we go straight back to Hoenderloo tomorrow, my darling? I have a list for the following day, but after that I'm free until after Christmas. We shall have the house to ourselves, Mama is going to Emma's and we are invited there for Christmas Day, so we shall have a day or so together, and at New Year, the whole family will come to us again, and I thought we might ask your mother and father as well...'

Britannia's eyes filled with tears. 'Oh, Jake, I'd love to go back to Hoenderloo—your mother doesn't mind?'

'She loves you, dearest, they all do.' He smiled at her. 'Are you going to cry? Do you want my handkerchief?'

She shook her head. 'I'm not crying, truly I'm not. Must I see anyone before I go?'

'Your Principal Nursing Officer said that she would be in her office until ten o'clock. What about your friends?'

'They'll be together in someone's room, having tea,' said Britannia. 'I can see them all at once and pack in ten minutes.'

'Then eat some of that cheese, my darling, and have another cup of this extremely strong tea and I'll take you back.'

The café had thinned of customers by now, the last of them had gone by the time Britannia had obediently gobbled down the toasted cheese. Ned came over with the bill and the professor paid with a handsome tip, and Ned, who was no fool, melted through the little door behind the counter and left them alone.

'Ready?' asked the professor, and came round to button her into her cape once more.

She looked up at him and smiled. 'We'll have to hurry.'

'You are quite right, my darling, as you so often are, but no one is going to hurry me for a moment.'

He put his arms round her and bent to kiss her, and no one, least of all Britannia, hurried him.